ISLAND OF THE CRABS

STEVEN J. TAYLOR

SEVERED PRESS
HOBART TASMANIA

ISLAND OF THE CRABS

WWW.SEVEREDPRESS.COM

ISBN: 978-1-922551-68-9

PROLOGUE

Jorge cut the engine and let the boat's momentum carry it forth until it crunched to a halt on the sand of the beach. His eyes scanned the island for movement, but everything was as silent and as still as if he had landed on the surface of the moon.

He waited a few moments, then cupped his hands to his mouth to yell.

"*Hola,*" he called, "*estoy aquí.*"

He was answered by complete silence. There was not even an insect chirp to be heard.

Jorge pulled off his worn old cap and wiped the sweat from his brow. His eyes darted left and right, searching, and hoping, for a sign of movement. But none came.

Jorge placed the cap back on his head and checked the time on his watch. He tapped his foot, the sound extraordinarily loud in this place of quiet, and then leaned over the side to examine the water. The water here was beautifully crystal clear, and the white sand gleamed underneath as clean as bleached paper. Jorge looked back up at the island and called out once more. Still nothing. He slapped the wheel and pursed his lips. Finally, he came to a decision. He clambered over the cracked windscreen of his boat, onto the bow deck before leaping onto the sandy beach.

As he walked up the beach, his eyes darted warily about. He did not like being on this island, and he did not want to stay here long.

As he reached the top of the beach, he spied the campsite ahead of him.

"*Hola,*" he called once more, "*estoy aquí.*"

But there was no movement about the camp. Jorge glanced nervously back to the beach, before turning and advancing towards the campsite.

There were bloodstains visible in the dirt long before he arrived at the camp. He scuffed them over to cover them with dirt. Something white glinted and caught his eye. He bent down and picked it up. A human tooth. He pocketed the find.

Closer to the camp, the blood patches were larger, but there were no signs of any bodies. He continued to scuff about the dirt, covering the dark patches on the ground.

He entered the campsite. A fire still gently smouldered in the centre, the dark coals glowing an evil red around the edges. Bags of food had been torn open and rubbish littered the camp. Blood stained the earth here too, and the tents were empty. Something very bad had happened here, and it did not surprise Jorge in the least.

Jorge placed his hands on his hips as he looked over the mess. He checked his watch. He had been here ten minutes. He should not stay here a long time, but he could not leave everything as it was. With a sigh, he bent down and started pulling the tent pegs out of the ground. He unclipped the poles, folded the tent down and rolled it up. This camping gear had been expensive, he was not going to just leave it here to rot.

Next, he tidied up the rubbish into bags. He collected the strewn clothes and replaced them into the backpacks. None of it would fit him or his family, but he could sell the clothes to a second-hand shop or better, give them to charity. One in five people in his country lived in poverty. The clothes should not go to waste.

Finally, he hurriedly loaded everything back onto his boat. He stood on the beach and took one last look back at the island. He would not search for the people he had left here two days earlier, because he knew he would not find people, only corpses, and he did not want to face the authorities and explain that.

He pushed his boat back from the shoreline before dexterously leaping up onto the bow deck. He clambered back over the windshield and down to the stern engine. As he pulled the rip cord to start it up, he took one last look at the island. He shook his head sombrely. It was a sad business, this. But people kept asking to come here. He always warned them, but that only made them push harder.

No more, Jorge decided. Too many have died. This was it. This would be the last time he brought people to this island.

Wistfully, Jorge turned to take his seat at the wheel. Nodding to affirm his resolve, he pushed the throttle forward, vowing never to return.

1

The bus rocked like a ship in a storm as the front wheel went through what must have been the hundredth pot hole of the last mile. Leigh tensed his muscles to avoid his head banging against the railing as he was thrown about like a rag doll in a playful puppy's mouth. Beside him, Andy laughed, throwing his head back in an exaggerated manner.

"You're enjoying this, aren't you?" Leigh asked, then braced as the back wheels of the bus passed through the pot hole causing the bus to rock wildly once more.

Leigh and Andy had given up their seats a while earlier to a pair of elderly women. There were no other empty seats on the bus, forcing them to stand on this bucking bronco. It had been a rough journey and Leigh's arm and leg muscles were starting to ache from the constant bracing and tensing. Leigh was a big guy and he worked out regularly, but this ride was a whole other challenge, and must have been testing the muscles that did not get the strengthening they needed from lifting weights.

Then again, this ride really was something beyond anything he had experienced before. It was the perfect formula for chaos; badly unkept roads with more holes than a slice of Swiss cheese, a bus with shoddy suspension and a driver that thought he was behind the wheel of a Formula One race car. It was all Leigh needed to cling to the handrail white knuckled as though clinging for dear life.

Whereas Leigh had gritted his teeth, Andy had smiled broadly. This is what he had lived for. Adventure. Going off the beaten track, exploring the unknown and going places where people rarely went for a holiday. That is how they had ended up on the island of Colón, part of an archipelago of islands on the northern tip of Panama.

It was a beautiful place, bearing all the hallmarks you would want in a Caribbean getaway. Hot, sunny days. Crystal clear ocean water. Stunning rainforests bursting with rare wildlife. Surf beaches. Swimming beaches. Friendly locals. Vibrant colours. Exotic foods. Bustling nightlife with, importantly, plenty of alcohol and cute local girls. It should be spoken of as one of the top travel destinations in the Caribbean, if only it stopped lazing itself in the sun and modernised.

But for two young Australian men like Leigh and Andy, visiting a place like this *before* it became big was the whole reason for coming. The bragging point at parties. The thing that you could say at any gathering and instantly be ten times more interesting. This point was especially important to Andy, who regarded himself as a 'social influencer'. He even referred to this as his profession when asked, despite working a boring, dead end retail job back home.

The bus hit another bump in the road and Andy let out a whoop of joy before laughing once more. If any of the locals thought his behaviour strange, they did not show it. Perhaps they were used to tourists reacting in such a way. Leigh glanced at them before frowning down at Andy.

"Oh, come on," Andy remarked, his voice light and airy, "you've been enjoying the bumps too."

"Are you kidding? I've almost hit my head five times now."

"That's your fault for being so tall. Besides, I wasn't referring to the ride. I was referring to the bumps. And the view."

Leigh frowned in confusion. Andy elaborated with a nod towards the back of the bus. Leigh's eyes widened and he felt heat rising to his cheeks and knew he was reddening. He leant close to Andy.

"Have I been that obvious?" he said in a voice close to a whisper.

"Oh yeah, you've barely taken your eyes off of her since you stood up."

Leigh grimaced, then surreptitiously glanced again to the back of the bus where she sat. She was blond, with hazel-green eyes and a freckled face. She had a nose piercing with a thin gold ring hanging from it. Her long hair flowed down across her tanned shoulders. She was thin, but had large breasts. She had a great body, and was unashamed to show it, riding the bus in just a bikini top and a pair of tight denim shorts.

Leigh had been mesmerised by her. The way she flicked her hair from her face. The gentle bouncing of her breasts as the bus rode the bumps of the road. He found it hard to look away.

She sat with a couple with whom she shared jokes and laughter. Leigh knew them for a couple, the man's arm draped casually across the girl's shoulders. They were both equally as blond, though less overt as they both wore T-shirts over their bathing suits.

"You're staring at her again," Andy said.

Leigh forced his eyes from the girl to give Andy another frown. Andy stared at his friend a moment, then huffed.

"Ok," Andy began again, "chances are, with her being on this bus at this time of day, she and her friends there are also staying on Bocas Town. I think we need to go over the ground rules, just in case we run into them again."

Leigh rolled his eyes. "Not this again," he said.

"Mate," Andy said, cutting him off, "you're shit at picking up girls. I'm going to keep going over these rules until you prove otherwise." Andy stopped, tilted his head forward and gave Leigh a squinty eyed examination. Andy then leaned back, pursed his lips. "You already think you're in love with her, don't you?"

"Andy, please..."

"Ah-ha, it's true," Andy said, taking one hand away from the handrail to wave his index finger as his friend. "You've already broken the first rule. Don't put her on a pedestal before you've even spoken to her."

Leigh looked away and started shaking his head. He wished he could pull his hands away from the handrails and cover his ears, but if he did that, he would probably wind up hitting his head or worse, falling over and landing in the lap of a seated passenger. The last thing those two old Panamanian women needed was a big guy like Leigh sitting on their lap.

"Andy, I don't want to go over this again. Not here, not now," Leigh remarked, trying to sound forceful without drawing the attention of the passengers on the bus. He gave Andy a hard look to reinforce his point.

Andy stared at him a moment longer before conceding.

"Fine. But I'm telling you, man, I don't want to see you continue to fuck these things up. You fall for these chicks before you've even spoken to them, then when you finally do get the courage to talk to them you already have this image of them being some virtuous angel that you won't even make a move. You hang around them like a puppy and then when you muster up the courage to tell her how you feel you find out she's getting dick from some other guy and you're already deeply entrenched in the friend zone."

Leigh took a hand away from the handrail and held his hand open, palm out, to Andy.

"Alright Andy, I know the lecture, you can stop now." The words came out harsher than Leigh had intended.

"I'm just saying Leigh…" Andy began, but was quickly cut off by the sudden, loud blasting of reggaeton through the speakers of the bus. The music was loud and distorted, and any attempts to continue the conversation over the cacophony would be pointless.

Leigh sighed and looked out the window, glad that the driver's intervention by switching on the radio had help him get out of a conversation he did not want to have. The radio regularly cracked and fizzed, but they must have been closing on Bocas Town if he was now getting a signal.

Leigh tried to resist the urge to glance to the back of the bus again. To glance at her. But the temptation was too strong, and his willpower too weak. He lifted his head and turned it slightly to the side to see her once more. She, too, had broken off her conversation with her friends and instead looked out the window. A shame, Leigh thought, he liked the way she laughed. Her smile.

Suddenly she looked up and caught his eye. He panicked, looking away quickly. Shit, he thought, she caught me staring at her. She probably thinks I'm some sort of weirdo now.

He dared another glance her way. She was looking at the window again. Phew, she was not watching him to see if he had been staring. It was ok. He looked away from her again, conscious not to look at her too much. Only a few more times before the ride ended.

2

It was after the fifth blast on his horn that the driver finally gave up and opened the doors of the bus. He shouted something neither of the two young Australians could understand, but the locals clearly got the message and soon everyone began slowly disembarking.

Andy looked up at Leigh and shrugged. "I guess this is as far as we go," he said.

They followed the slow line towards the door, and as Leigh descended the steps, he got his bearings. They were two streets away from where the bus was supposed to drop them, but a truck had parked ahead and blocked the narrow road. Two workers, clearly nonplussed by the red-faced, obscenity-shouting bus driver and honking cars from the traffic jam they had caused, were unloading crates of soft drinks and alcohol from the truck and carrying them into a nearby bar. Judging from the speed of their movements, they were in no hurry to finish the job any time soon.

Andy soon joined him, dropping his bag on the ground next to Leigh's feet. Leigh heard the bleeping of Andy's camera as Andy started scrolling through his photos for the day. Andy preferred using his camera over his phone for anything he was posting online. He always claimed the camera delivered higher quality images and video than any phone ever could.

Leigh looked at the bus, watching the passengers disembark. He waited for her, just to get another glimpse. He did not have to wait long for her to appear in the doorway. She was distracted, talking as she started walking down the steps. Leigh had only registered she was not speaking English when her thong caught and she almost fell. He took a step forward, thinking he might need to catch her, be her knight in shining armour, when she regained herself and put one barefoot onto the road. She climbed out and unwedged her thong, laughing and chatting with her friends, having not noticed him at all.

He watched the trio walk off, wondering what language they had spoken. He could not pick it. It was certainly not one they had learnt in school. He was watching them walk off when he felt Andy's hand slap him on the back before wrapping over his shoulder.

"I'm normally not an arse man," Andy began in a voice dripping with sleaze, "but her rear end certainly tells me I need to rethink that position."

Leigh rolled his eyes and shrugged Andy's hand from his shoulder.

"I'm going back to the hostel," Leigh said in a matter-of-fact tone. "I need a shower to wash this salt off. You coming?"

"Nah, I'm going to go to the internet café and upload some pictures. I want to make sure my followers have some cool shots to wake up to back home."

Andy stopped and held the camera screen first to Leigh.

"Check out that shot."

Leigh looked at the photo of a starfish, its bright blue colouring contrasting against the white sand and clearly visible through the pristine clear waters at Starfish Beach. It was a good picture, really showing the beauty of the place that they had visited. What it did not show was Andy had spent one hour in the water looking for the perfect photo and the next half of the day at the bar. But, hey, that was the life of an influencer, was it not?

"It's great," Leigh said without enthusiasm. "Should I wait for you back at the hostel?"

"Yeah, I'll only be an hour or so."

"Right, see you later then."

Leigh turned and started down the road when he heard Andy call his name again.

"Leigh," Andy called, "keep asking around, will you?"

Leigh took a deep breath in, and then huffed it out as he turned.

"Let me guess. You want me to keep asking about Crab Island?" he called back. His voice carried an edge of exasperation.

"Yeah, exactly. Someone around here must know about it."

Leigh frowned and ran his fingers through his hair.

"I don't think it exists, man. We've looked at all the maps and it's not there. We've asked everyone we've met since we arrived and no one's ever heard of it before. You're chasing a myth."

Andy shook his head. "It's no myth, mate. It's real. Keep asking, someone will know it."

"Righto," Leigh called back with no conviction. He turned and trudged on.

Crab Island. It was all Andy could talk about. It was supposed to be some strange, legendary place that existed somewhere out here in the Bocas del Toro province of Panama. Andy was convinced it was an island somewhere in this archipelago, but even those locals that knew the islands well denied its existence. They had even searched the internet for clues to back it up, but the web was strangely devoid of any references.

Leigh had long stopped believing Crab Island existed. He became convinced it was just an urban legend, no more real than Big Foot or the Loch Ness monster. When he told this to Andy, Andy only doubled down on his belief.

"It exists," he would insist. "It's hidden, but it's real. We just haven't looked in the right places or spoken to the right people yet. We just have to keep looking and asking. We'll find it, trust me."

Yet despite Andy's assurances and belief, there was still no tangible evidence that such a place existed. Leigh had started believing they would have better luck if they instead turned their attention in looking for the cup of Christ. At least there was some evidence that it had once existed!

But Leigh, at least, understood why Andy was so desperate to find this mythical place. Andy was still new to the influencer game, and his following was not that big. Not yet. He wanted to go big on it, start extracting big dollars from advertisers eager to place their goods in his posts. He wanted to turn it not just into a living, but get rich from it too. And what was Andy's logic for how he would achieve this magical goal? By travelling to the most obscure place in the world and being the first person on social media to document a visit on the fabled Crab Island.

What was so special about this place? Leigh could not even answer the question himself. There was a vague mythos about the place, it was something of a legend that people 'in the know' knew existed, but could not actually tell you anything tangible about. And that is what made it so attractive.

What Leigh did know was that it was supposed to be something of an 'adventure tourist' type place. Akin to visiting Chernobyl. Only Chernobyl was real, and everyone knew where it was and what the risks were going there. Crab Island was something else entirely, and more and more Leigh began feeling that maybe it was better that Andy did not find his Holy Grail after all. Something as secret as this must be secret for a reason.

Leigh checked his watch and saw he had plenty of time on his hands before they went out. He decided to take the longer route back to the hostel and walk along the shoreline route.

Bocas Town was a small town that nestled on the south-east corner of the island of Colón. It was the capital of the archipelago region, home to the airport and all of the central tour companies, and it was the first stop on any trip to this part of the world.

Leigh and Andy had arrived last Thursday, and today was their fourth full day on the island. This had given Leigh plenty of time to get his bearings, and he was starting to get to know Bocas Town with the same familiarity as his own neighbourhood back home in Melbourne. He much preferred walking along the shoreline streets of Bocas Town to the inner-city. Despite the overly dressy tourist attraction-ness of the shoreline, the streets just had far more life to them. Buildings were painted brighter, the streets cleaner and the line of cafés, restaurants and bars all spilled spicy food smells and exotic dance music into the streets giving the area a unique vibrancy.

They had spent most of their first two days here exploring Bocas Town. Andy looked for the perfect postcard shots to post on social media while Leigh soaked in the atmosphere of the place. And when Andy was busy in some internet café fulfilling his social media requirements, Leigh applied himself to learning the difference in styles of music and how to dance to them. From cumbia to reggae to salsa, he was starting to get his head and clumsy feet around the correct moves. The only thing Leigh was failing to pick up was Spanish, but he was never good at languages in school so that was no real surprise.

As Leigh walked down the street, he was again drawn into the atmosphere of Bocas Town. He bought some *carimañolas*, stuffed yuca fritters, from a street vendor and snacked on these as he walked. He stopped outside a restaurant and browsed the displayed menu outside when he heard a voice call out.

"Hey," the voice shouted, "hey, *gringo*. You, big man."

He turned to the strange calls to see a dark-skinned man with an eye-patch running up the street towards him. He recognised the man immediately. His name was Juan. He and Andy had shared drinks with him the night before. Andy had bought him a few rounds in an attempt to get information on Crab Island. Juan knew nothing of it but promised to ask around. He was good company, and during the night Andy jokingly started calling him 'one eyed Juan' and later, for fun, 'Juan eyed one' to see if the man noticed. Juan either failed to note it or chose to ignore it. Perhaps the latter, since Andy kept buying him drinks all night.

Leigh raised his hand to wave and waited for Juan. Juan arrived breathing heavily, sweat glinting from the sun off his dark skin. He bent over onto his haunches to catch his breath, before standing up again.

"I have found the Crab Island you want," he said at last, a triumphant smile on his face.

"You know where it is?" Leigh asked.

"No," Juan declared. "I found a man who takes people there. Very hard to find. Very secret. But this man, he knows. He can take you there."

For a moment Leigh paused. No doubt had Andy been here he would have been jumping for joy right now, but Leigh felt oddly disappointed. For a moment he considered the mystery may have been the allure, and that finding the enigma would somehow take away its glossy appeal.

"Great," said Leigh, his words a contradiction to how he felt, "where do we find this guy?"

"I will introduce you. Come to Barco Hundido tonight."

Leigh nodded and bid Juan farewell. He knew Barco Hundido well. It was a waterfront bar, with the main bar area and dancefloor built out over the water on stilts with views that looked out to nearby Carenero Island. They had good pizzas there too. It was a good place.

Leigh stared back at the menu without seeing it as his mind reeled with the news. Crab Island. It was real. He took another bite of his fritter and turned, thinking over all of the things Andy had said about the place. Its legend. Its myth.

And now he knew it was real, he had to ask himself another important question. If this was an extreme tourist destination, did that make it dangerous? And if so, did he even want to go there?

He pushed the thought aside. Best not dwell on it. After all, as soon as Andy heard the news, he doubted he would be given any choice in the matter anyway.

3

Andy was as excited as a child on Christmas morning when he heard the news. He could barely contain himself, and Leigh imagined he could see the dollar signs light up in Andy's eyes, such was his cartoonish behaviour. Andy was so distracted Leigh even had to herd him into the shower as his jaw jabbered endlessly with stories of Crab Island and how he was going to be the first influencer to visit and post pictures of the place.

"Think of it," Andy said after coming out, staring off into the distance, blissfully unaware his towel had fallen to the floor giving everyone present full view of the family jewels, "I, Andy Hudson, am about to go down in internet folklore as the man to first post a report on Crab Island."

"Yeah, yeah," Leigh replied, throwing a pair of shorts at his friend. Andy caught them without looking.

"You're not listening Leigh. This will make me big. Like, Pewdiepie big. Do you have any idea how big that is?"

Leigh sighed and looked away. Sometimes there was no getting through to Andy. Not when he was on a tangent like this. He watched a couple of girls leave the room, giggling as they left.

"Look," Leigh said, interrupting Andy's latest fame fantasy monologue, "any chance you can put some fucking clothes on? We're all getting tired of seeing your dick."

Andy stopped and looked down to examine himself. "What's wrong with my dick? It's a beautiful dick."

"Then post it on social media," Leigh replied. He threw a t-shirt at Andy and got up.

"Where are you going?" Andy asked as he pulled the shirt over his head.

"Downstairs. I'll see you there. When you're dressed."

Andy came down surprisingly quickly once Leigh had left the room. He was checking his camera as he dismounted the final stairs before looking up to find Leigh.

"Right, so where are we going to meet this guy?" he asked.

"Barco Hundido."

Andy rolled his eyes. "Barco Hundido again? I've already posted pics from there."

"Not everything is a social media moment."

"It is when you have an audience hungry for new content."

Andy made them walk a different way to Barco Hundido, trying streets they had not previously walked down hoping to find something new and post worthy.

They arrived at Barco Hundido at seven o'clock. The bar was already starting to fill, and the music had not been turned up to party level just yet as most of the patrons were here for dinner. They ordered pizzas and beers, and Leigh tried to listen to the *rock en español* over Andy's endless chattering.

As Leigh was lifting his second piece of pizza over to his plate, he noticed three new patrons enter from the corner of his eyes. He suddenly felt Andy kick him hard under the table.

"She's here," Andy hissed between his teeth. "Your Madonna is here. Maybe we both get what we want tonight, eh?"

Leigh looked up at the three blondes that had just entered the room to see it was true. She was here. The girl from the bus. He watched as she and her friends sat at a table at the opposite end of the room. She was dressed casually in short denim shorts and a loose-fitting pink top. She laughed and flicked her hair and Leigh again found himself transfixed.

"Hey moron, stop staring," Andy hissed.

Leigh looked to his friend and again found himself reddening.

"Jesus," Andy said shaking his head, "you really need to learn how to play it cool with chicks."

"You're not going to run through the rules again, are you?" Leigh asked disdainfully.

Andy looked at Leigh with the pity a teacher would give a failing student at school. Finally, Andy let out an exaggerated sigh and raised his hands in mock surrender.

"Fine. I'll lay off and let you do it your way. Just don't come running to me when some other guy is balls deep into her pussy and she's telling you she prefers the two of you to just be friends. OK?"

Leigh gave Andy a dark look then turned away. He took a long drink from his beer, then slammed the bottle on the table.

"I'll talk to her tonight. You watch. I'll win her over my way."

Andy stared at Leigh a moment before nodding ascent. "Sure."

The topic seemingly over, Andy started to again become restless. His eyes darted with eagerness at every new patron that entered, and with each passing moment he became more and more aggravated.

"Fuck," he said as two more strangers entered, "where the hell is Juan eyed one at? You don't think he was bullshitting you, do you?"

"He seemed genuine about it."

"Shit, I wish he'd hurry up."

While Andy spent his time watching patrons enter, Leigh was busy planning his opening line. He had no idea what to say. 'Just be yourself' was what everyone always told him. Be himself? Being himself only made girls like him as a friend. Should he be like Andy? No. For starters, he doubted he could pull it off with any degree of sincerity. And for seconds, he sometimes felt that Andy came off as a bit of an arrogant dickhead. Granted, he had success with girls being that way, but Leigh just could not find it in himself to be like that.

It was not long after the pizza had finished and the two boys had emptied their third beers that Andy suddenly got up and made his way to the entrance. Leigh was woken from his reverie to see Juan had entered with another man.

The second man was older, maybe forty or fifty years of age, and had deeply tanned skin marked with spots. He was skinny, extremely so, and his clothes hung like loose sails around a mast on a boat. His eyebrows were a thick black and hung heavily over his dark eyes that darted about the room distrustfully. He looked out of place amongst the young crowd at the bar, and did not seem comfortable with the idea either. As he turned, Leigh saw a thick scar running from behind the man's ear, down his neck and under the collar of his shirt.

Andy was quick to greet them. The man shook Andy's hand without smiling, and Juan directed them to a table in the corner away from other patrons. Andy turned and waved for

Leigh to join them. Leigh waved his hand to decline. He had other plans. He was going to approach her.

Leigh went to the bar and ordered another beer. Slowly he turned, taking the room in. The three blondes sat talking. In front of them were glasses of *ron ponche*, the popular cocktail in these parts. Leigh and Andy had tried them on the first night. They tasted a bit like eggnog. Leigh was not a fan.

But perhaps that could be his opening to speak with them? *Ron Ponche* eh? That's such a strong drink, they should consider calling it *ron punchy*, because it packs such a punch.

Ugh. No. That was terrible. He would be laughed out of the bar if he opened with that.

He took another sip as he thought what he could say, but like an impotent man, he kept shooting blanks. He smirked to himself. Now that was funny. Not something he could use as an opener, but still funny.

He took another sip. He was already halfway through the beer and still he stood by the bar like an idiot. He cursed himself for delaying. Time to shit or get off the pot.

He walked over to their table. He tried to swagger, but felt ungainly in doing so and quickly resumed his normal walk. He glanced to the corner where Andy was in deep conversation with Juan and the second man. He looked back at the table. None of them had even glanced his way yet.

He sat down at the table opposite them. They broke off their conversation and turned their eyes at him questioningly.

"Hi," was all Leigh could say.

"Hi," she replied with a smile.

"I…" Blank. Shit, shit, shit, shit. He was floundering.

"I think I saw you on the bus today," she said, saving him. Her voice was musical and thickly accented, though Leigh still struggled to place what country she could be from.

"Really? Uh… I mean yes," Leigh answered, "I was just about to say the same thing."

She gave him a quizzical smile. "So, where did you go today?"

"Up to Starfish Beach."

"Oh," she said raising an eyebrow, "we were there too. Funny we didn't see you there."

"My friend Andy and I spent most of the day at the bar."

"At the bar? You went to such a beautiful beach and you spent the day at the bar?"

Leigh reddened with embarrassment, even though it had not been his idea, he had gone along with it and missed out. He had no real answer, and the silence started getting awkward so he decided to introduce himself.

"My name's Bartlett by the way. Leigh Bartlett."

"That's a very James Bond-like introduction. My name's Hoovler. Inge Hoovler. And these are my friends, Dirk and Marianne."

Leigh smiled a greeting to them. They nodded in return, but the dull look in their eyes betrayed how little interest they had in meeting him.

"If you don't mind me asking," Leigh continued, "where are you all from?"

"We are from Nederland."

"Ah, the land of clogs and windmills," Leigh said.

Dirk snorted and looked away, and Leigh realised just how stupid what he had just said was. He looked at Inge, but she still retained a half smile on her face.

"And what about you, Leigh, where are you from?"

"I'm an Australian."

"Oh, throw another shrimp on the barbie mate," Inge said in a terrible mock Australian accent.

Leigh smiled. She had a sense of humour. That was good.

"Well played. I guess we all have our national cliches. Sorry about the clog and windmill remark. It just came out."

Inge smiled. "That's ok. Dirk's only upset because you forgot to mention the tulips."

That drew another derisive snort from Dirk, but it did ease the uncomfortable feeling that was growing inside Leigh. Despite the shaky introduction, they soon settled into a smooth conversation and even Dirk and Marianne started joining in. A few drinks later Leigh felt he had integrated himself into their little friendship bubble. He learned that they had only just arrived in Panama two days ago, and that this archipelago was their first destination of a wide-ranging tour of the country. They talked about plans of places they intended to visit in the islands.

"Tomorrow we are going to Nivida," Inge said

"Oh, what a coincidence, so am I," Leigh lied. He did not even know what Nivida was. "What company did you book your trip through?"

When Inge said the name, he made a mental note of it. He would try and book the same tour first thing in the morning.

"Same again," he lied once more, "perhaps we'll be on the same boat."

That's when Inge leaned forward conspiratorially to talk to Leigh.

"It's going to be hilarious. Marianne hates animals. She once freaked out because Dirk's mother's cat tried to sit in her lap. She almost threw the poor animal out of a fifth-floor apartment window just to get it away from her. Can you imagine how she will be in a cave swarming with bats?"

Bats? Just what had Leigh signed himself up for?

A fresh beer was then placed on the table in front of Leigh. The hand then lifted to give him a slap on the back. Andy slid into the seat beside him with a broad grin on his face.

"It's all organised. We leave Tuesday and camp on Crab Island for two nights, back in time for filthy Friday."

Andy was giddy with excitement, only Leigh was less pleased to see him. He hid it, but Leigh was annoyed at Andy's presence. He was happy in his new quartet, with no real competition for Inge's attention. Now he had to duke it out with his alpha male mate.

Andy held his beer out. "Cheers," he shouted, gulping down most of the beer in one.

Leigh took a sip from his whilst he tried not to scowl. As he lowered it from his mouth, Andy clinked his bottle against Leigh's and downed another mouthful. Leigh just stared at him.

"What?" Andy asked, then turned to the other occupants of the table, surprise showing on his face as if just now noticing them for the first time. "G'day, I'm Andy," he said, and thrust his hand out to shake each of their hands in turn. They each introduced themselves to him.

Just after introductions, it was Dirk who spoke up.

"You said something about going to a Crab Island? I've read up about this whole area and I've never seen or heard that name before. What is it?"

"*Si,*" Andy replied in his poorly accented Spanish. "*Isla Cangrejo*. Crab Island. It's this top-secret place only a few people know about, and me and Leigh here just got an exclusive ticket to the place."

Dirk leaned forward suddenly quite interested.

"What's on this island? What makes it so special?"

"Well, that's the thing. No one really knows about this place, but it's meant to be one of the most extreme places to visit in the world."

Dirk was listening intently and it was obvious he was interested.

"Do you lot want to join us? Splitting the cost will make it easier for us if you're keen?"

"Is there going to be crabs?" Marianne asked with a scowl.

"How much did it cost?" Leigh asked before Andy had a chance to answer her.

Andy turned and bit his lip.

"A thousand bucks U.S.," he answered.

"One thousand dollars?" Leigh replied with exasperation. "Jesus, Andy. Are you sure this is real? He's not just taking you for a ride, is he?"

"No, he's legit."

Andy took a sip of his beer and then turned back to Leigh. Leigh frowned thoughtfully.

"He's legit. Trust me." Andy then turned back to the Dutch trio opposite him. "What do you lot reckon? You want in? It'll be like nothing you've ever done before. You'll be bragging to your mates about it for years to come."

Dirk seemed genuinely intrigued, but the two girls seemed doubtful.

"C'mon," Andy urged, "it's a once in a lifetime thing and it's as rare as the dodo. You'll be in elite company of visitors."

Dirk looked at the girls, evaluating their faces before looking back to Andy.

"We'll think about it," he said.

Andy finished his beer and slammed his bottle on the table.

"Right then, I'm in a good mood. Let's get some more drinks and get this fucking party started."

4

"Come on Andy, get up already," Leigh pleaded, "the boat leaves in half an hour."

Andy groaned, squinting up at Leigh who hovered over him with a stressed look on his face.

"Where are we going?" he croaked.

"I've told you four times already. Nivida."

Andy grimaced and closed his eyes once more. "What is Nivida?"

Leigh threw his hands in the air in exasperation. "For the fourth time, it's a bat cave."

"Will Batman be there?"

"That joke wasn't funny the first three times, what makes you think it would be funny now?"

"Fine," Andy said, and let out an audible groan as he raised himself into a seated position on the bed. "I just don't get why we're going there."

"Because I told Inge we were going with them."

"Aha," Andy said, starting to come to life at last. "Inge. Inge Hoovler." He flashed a cheeky grin at Leigh and then put on a silly voice. "Inge Hoovler, Inge Hoolver, Inge Hoovler. Sounds like something that Swedish chef on the Muppets would say while waving a whisk about."

"That ain't funny, man. And, for the record, she's Dutch."

Andy held up his hands in mock surrender. "Hey, sorry man. Didn't mean to insult your future bride there."

"Jesus," Leigh cursed, "just get ready, will you?"

Andy pulled himself up off the bed and staggered into the bathroom, leaving the door open so everyone in the room could hear him piss. He washed his hands, splashing water on his face to break the fogginess of his hangover. Feeling better, he staggered back into the room where Leigh waited.

"What's so special about this bat cave anyway?"

"It's one of the top tourist attractions around here. You'd know this already if you did some proper research about the archipelago and hadn't focused all your attention into finding Crab Island."

"Whatever," Andy groaned and began to slowly dress.

They almost missed the boat. They had to run a couple of blocks to make it, and even then it was a close call. One of the crew had already started untying the boat from the jetty when they arrived. He seemed reluctant to, but after a quick few words, he let them on.

Leigh quickly spotted his new friends and made his way over to them. They gave a friendly greeting when they saw him.

"We thought you wouldn't make it," Inge said as they came close.

In response, Leigh rolled his eyes and pointed his thumb back at Andy who trailed in his wake.

"A bit hungover there are you, Andy?" Inge called.

"You could say that," said Andy, starting to look a little pale. "And I'm not sure a ride on a rocking boat is the best thing for me right now but, fuck it, here I am."

Inge laughed. Leigh really liked her laugh. She turned back to Leigh and held out a closed fist.

"I have a present for you. Give me your hand."

Leigh's pulse quickened as he held out an open palm and watched her drop a small item in it. He looked down to see she had given him a keyring with two small wooden clogs on it. He gave a short laugh.

She smiled and shrugged. "It's a memento for next time you meet a Dutch person not to think of the first cliché that comes to mind."

He smiled again. He was starting to really like her.

The boat ride to Bastimentos Island, the home of the Nivida caves, was pleasant. The waters were gentle, sheltered as they were in the archipelago, and there was a coolness to the air that made the trip enjoyable. Andy lay down on one seat and placed his cap over his face in an attempt to sleep while Leigh continued to fertilise his growing acquaintance with Inge and her friends.

Upon arriving at Bastimentos Island, they transferred to a second boat at the entrance to an inland channel. The channel ran inland through a mangrove forest. The area was rich with vegetation and wildlife. Strange but brightly coloured birds fluttered between trees, exhibiting their vibrant plumage and weirdly alien calls. There were three-toed sloths dangling lazily from overhead branches and on more than one occasion the travellers spotted the white-faced Capuchin Monkeys swinging between trees or staring down at them with curious eyes.

"They are so little and cute," Inge remarked as they passed a cluster in one tree, "I wish I could have one as a pet."

"No thanks," responded Marianne.

Leigh then remembered what Inge had said the night before. Marianne did not like animals. He shook his head. If she was that afraid, how on earth did they convince her to enter a cave filled with bats?

Leigh had his attention drawn by Andy snapping his fingers.

"Leigh, I need you here. Get some photos of me with those monkeys in the background."

Leigh pushed himself up and slunk over to grab Andy's camera from him. He was a little annoyed by the finger clicking and rude asking so he deliberately framed some of the photos badly. A small, but satisfying revenge.

At the end of the boat trip, the tourists were then required to hike down a path to get to the cave itself. It was muddy and slippery, but easy enough to traverse if you concentrated on where you put your feet. On more than one occasion Andy interrupted Leigh's conversation with Inge to order him in a clipped tone to take a photo of him with a monkey or sloth in the background.

"Why does he insist on getting so many photos of himself?" Inge asked Leigh when he returned to her side.

"Oh, he's an influencer on social media," Leigh answered, "he'll only put up the ones he likes so he ends up taking a lot."

"Oh, that makes sense. I just thought he was really into himself."

He actually is, Leigh thought to himself.

After half an hour they reached the cave entrance. The tour guide started handing out headlamps and after a few more posed photographs, they plunged into the darkness of the cave.

The roof of the cave stretched high above them, and as their eyes adjusted to the gloom, it soon became apparent that the rock surface above was alive with movement. Hundreds of small, dangling stalactites shifted and moved about. Small shapes flitted about in the darkness, and the occasional cheep of a bat was heard. Something flew past Marianne. She did not see it but knew from the sound of leathery flapping wings and the wind on her face. She squawked and clutched Dirk's hand hard, leaning close to him.

"This is cool," Andy remarked, "but no good for photos. Any chance we can get closer to them?"

The guide shook his head and moved on. Soon they came to an area of the cave where they needed to walk into the water. They followed the guide in, and in a short time the water was waist deep. Their progress slowed as they pushed on through the water. Andy stopped the group and insisted that Leigh took a photo of him. Leigh lined up the shot and clicked. There was a bright, blinding flash from the camera. Suddenly there was a great disturbance above them. A great cacophony of bat squeaks echoed through the cave as hundreds of the creatures suddenly took flight.

Within seconds, the air about them was alive with shapes and movement. Everywhere around them bats swooped and dived in a maelstrom of flapping wings and bat squeaks, lit up vividly by the narrow beams of their headlamp torches. Red eyes glinted in the lights, and small sharp white teeth glowed sinisterly every time they opened their mouths. Shadows danced and flickered, creating dramatic and frightening shadows everywhere.

"Stand still," yelled the guide over the noise.

Leigh froze as the bats fluttered about him. A wing brushed his head, causing him to jump. He tried to focus his eyes, but there was too much movement and too many shapes flitting past that his mind failed to process it all. In a moment he saw a bat lit starkly in his headlamp headed straight at his face. He raised his hands and braced, but the impact never came.

"I can't handle this," Marianne whimpered, clutching onto Dirk tightly. Her muscles were taut and stressed.

Inge crouched slowly into the water, making herself a smaller target.

A bat landed in Marianne's hair and she instantly screamed and started shaking her head about.

"Get it out, get it out, get it out," she yelled. She whipped her head about and the bat only became further entangled in her hair. The bat panicked and began lashing out with its teeth and claws. "It's attacking me. Help," she cried.

"Hold still," Dirk ordered, unable to offer any support while she panicked.

Her headlamp fell and splashed into the water as she screamed again.

Dirk thrust his hands into her hair and grabbed at the small shape. As he wrapped his fingers around the soft bundle, a sharp pain lanced through his fingers. He jerked at the shape, pulling not only the bat but a handful of hair, causing a greater scream from his girlfriend.

"Stop," ordered the guide, who had made his way slowly over.

Dirk pulled away and watched as the guide carefully untangled the bat from Marianne's hair. It was barely moving as the guide held it in his open palm, and Dirk realised he might have crushed it as he pulled it free.

Marianne leaned into Dirk, sobbing onto his shoulder.

"Just stay still and wait until they all calm," the guide ordered grumpily.

Within five minutes the storm of flying bats eased. Marianne still mumbled quietly into Dirk's shoulder. Inge stood up, her wet clothes clinging to her shapely figure. Leigh looked about, then waded over to Andy.

"Mate, you realise your headlamp lights up the exact thing you are looking at?"

"What?" Andy answered before realising his torch lit up Inge's wet T-shirt clinging sensually around her breasts. "Ah, sorry mate," he said turned away.

Leigh watched Andy walk away, his headlamp burning brightly on the centre of Andy's back.

5

Dirk let out a long sigh as he thumbed his way through the music collection he held on his phone. He was not in the mood for Eurodance, but that was all that he had stored. It would have to do for now. Eventually he chose a track and leaned back against the wall behind him.

On the bed in front of him sat Marianne and Inge. As soon as they had arrived back at the hostel, Marianne had dived into her backpack for the first aid kit she had packed. The small bat, now sadly dead due to Dirk's rough hands, had made quite a few scratches on Marianne's back in their mutual panicked state. Inge was now dabbing disinfectant onto the wounds.

Dirk closed his eyes and let the music wash over him.

All through the boat ride home he had been in deep conversation with Andy about Crab Island. Despite his disdain for surprises and mystery, Dirk could not help but be intrigued by the prospect of going there. It would be something he could hold over his friends back home. A card he had that they did not.

Dirk and Marianne had been together since the start of high school. Marianne was the only girl he had ever been with, and he was determined that it would remain that way for the rest of his life. His friends, though, were not tied down and always lorded it over him that they were enjoying their youth better than him by experiencing more women than he was. Time and again he watched his friends pick up girls in nightclubs and take them home. He was not jealous, he had all he needed, Marianne, and could not imagine his life being any other way than with her, but the constant teasing from his friends for having more 'life experience' by having more women did irk him.

Crab Island could change all that. If Crab Island was the experience that Andy made it out to be, then he would have a once in a lifetime experience he could hold over them. Life experience was not just sex, it was adventure, something which Crab Island promised in abundance. And, if it was as hard to find as Andy had made out, it was possible that they could search and never find it. It would be something he had that they could never match.

He sighed again. Unfortunately, it all depended on Inge and Marianne. He supposed he could go alone with Andy and Leigh and leave the two girls behind, but he did not think it would go down well. Besides, he wanted to be beside Marianne for the whole trip. This was the first time they had travelled overseas together. So yes, he would need to convince Marianne to go too. But after her experience in the bat cave today, she was unlikely to want to go to some mysterious place that was wild with animals. But was it wild? Details from Andy were sketchy, but the general consensus seemed to be that it would be known for its crabs. It said it in the name after all.

He opened his eyes to study her. What lever could he pull?

Marianne and Inge were smiling now and Inge gave Marianne a playful slap. He stopped the music to listen to the girls talk. They were talking about the two Australian guys and giggling. He rolled his eyes. He knew at some point on this trip it was bound to happen. Inge's break up with Martin, and his subsequent withdrawal from this trip, was bound to end in her having a holiday fling.

From what Dirk could gather, Inge liked both Leigh and Andy, and both of the Australian guys had taken a liking to her. It was only a matter of time. But who would she fuck? Would it be the bigger and more muscular Leigh, or would it be the good-looking Andy? That seemed to be the topic of conversation now, with Marianne acting as though she had as much vested interest in the outcome as Inge did. He smiled at her need to live vicariously through her friend.

Suddenly, it came to him. He pulled the headphones from his ears and leaned forward.

"You know," he said, trying to be as casual about it as he could, "going to Crab Island with them might be the perfect way to hook up."

The girls stopped and turned to him with their eyebrows raised.

"I don't think so," Inge said. "If I hook up with one, it gets awkward for the other and he becomes a third wheel."

"You're here with us and you're not a third wheel," Dirk pointed out.

"Yeah, but that would be different. Besides, I wouldn't go there alone. Not without you two."

"Then we should go as well. All of us together," Dirk said.

Marianne's smiled faded on her face as she studied Dirk. She looked away and took a deep breath.

"*Nu komt de aap uit de mouw.* Now we get to the truth of it. You were just looking for an excuse to jump in and push us in that direction. It's you who wants to go with them, isn't it, Dirk?" she asked.

His face flushed. "Yeah, I do."

Unconsciously, Marianne started to gently touch the scratches the bat gave her today. She was thinking. He knew her touching there was not a good sign. She was thinking about the animals she may encounter.

"Are you sure this 'Crab Island' is everything he says it is? He's not just dicking out of his neck?"

Dirk smiled. He loved that expression. It was very Dutch.

"True, he might be making it all up. But he might not be either, and if it is true, then I want to go. I want something like that to take home and tell everyone about. What's the worst that could happen if he's wrong? You spend two days on the beach on some remote island, which we would probably be doing here anyway."

Marianne frowned indecisively and turned to Inge.

"And what about you? Do you want to go as well?"

Inge smiled like the Cheshire cat.

"Well, it would be nice to spend some more time with the guys. And you'd want to come, would you? Just to see who I hook up with? Will it be Andy? Will it be Leigh? Or," she leaned in close to Marianne, "will it be both at the same time?"

Marianne's eyes went wide and she squealed. Dirk rolled his eyes. Inge burst out laughing, but went red in the process. Dirk looked at her and wondered how much of a joke that really was.

When they finally calmed down, he spoke up. "So, it's confirmed then? We go to Crab Island?"

Marianne cleared her throat and wiped the smile from her face. She sucked on her teeth a moment while she felt the scratches on her back once more.

"Ok, we'll go. I'm only doing this for you two. Not me. So, if there are any animals on this island, you need to keep them away from me. Deal?"

"Deal!" Dirk and Inge answered in unison.

It was decided then. They would go to Crab Island. He smiled, leaned back against the wall and placed the earbuds back in his ears. He thumbed through the tracks on his phone again. He needed to find a banger to fit his sudden good mood.

6

Leigh was excited and relieved when Dirk showed up at their hostel to confirm that all three of them would join him and Andy on the trip to Crab Island. He had laid a lot of groundwork with Inge, and was worried that someone else might step into the breach and sweep her up whilst he and Andy were away.

They all met early the next morning to withdraw money from the bank and buy supplies for the trip. In the agreement Andy had struck, the cost of the trip would cover the boat ride to the island and the rental of the camping equipment and firewood. All food and drink would need to be bought separately. As they shopped, Leigh found another reason to be happy with the inclusion of their new friends. They selected an array of fruits, vegetables and meats to take along. They would eat well. If it had just been up to him and Andy, they would only have bought cans of beans and beer and spent the whole two days on the island drinking and farting.

It was close to noon when they arrived at the dock for their boat ride. Leigh recognised the dark tanned man with heavy eyebrows and livid scar that Andy had spoken to at the bar. Andy rushed forward to greet him with a broad grin on his face. Contrastingly, the other man's face remained flat and emotionless.

"Jorge, these are my friends who are coming with me."

The man introduced as Jorge nodded a greeting but his face showed no emotion. He turned to Andy.

"Do you have money?"

Andy smiled politely at his bluntness, before digging into his pockets to retrieve the US dollars that they had withdrawn from the bank. Jorge counted through the bills quickly before pocketing them.

"And you are sure you want to go?"

"Too bloody right we are."

Jorge frowned and Leigh stepped forward.

"He means yes, we are." Not everyone understood Andy's Aussie slang.

Jorge nodded slowly and pointed towards his boat.

The boat was old and dilapidated. Rust smeared its sides, and the rear mounted engine looked to be hanging by a thread. There was enough room for the driver and eight people to sit along two bench seats. The cushions that lined the bench seats had split open along the corners, and one section of the exposed padding was stained red. The driver's seat was mounted behind a worn steering wheel and cracked window. In the centre of the boat were canvas bags and tied bundles of wood.

"That's the boat?" Marianne asked.

Andy smiled and shrugged, before turning to throw his bag in the back.

Leigh looked at the boat doubtfully. He felt like again asking Andy if he trusted this man, but one look at Andy's joy-filled face told him what the answer would be before the question was even asked. Leigh pursed his lips and hoped for the best.

Marianne shared a glance with Dirk, who also shrugged and moved forward to put his bag in. She stared a moment before following.

They all loaded their supplies and bags onto the boat. Jorge made no attempt to help. He only watched on with impassive eyes.

As everyone started taking their seats, Andy jumped up.

"Hold up," he cried, "I need to take and post one last picture before we set off on our intrepid adventure. Jorge, will you do the honours?"

Jorge frowned at first, unsure the meaning Andy was trying to convey by waving his phone at him. But as they mimed, he got the idea. He climbed back onto the dock as the group of five gathered in the centre of the boat and posed. Dirk hugged Marianne from behind. Leigh rested his arm on Andy's shoulder. Leigh liked showing he was bigger than Andy, especially when he could do it on Andy's social media feed. Andy gave the camera a double thumbs up, and Inge squatted between the two pairs. There was a click, and Jorge handed the phone back to Andy.

"Nice framing," Andy exclaimed, "if I ever need to replace Leigh, I'll keep you in mind, Jorge. This is a good photo except..."

"Except what?" asked Dirk. "The photo looks good to me."

Andy took a deep breath and looked at Dirk out of the corner of his eyes. "Well," Andy began contemplatively, "what if you weren't in the photo, Dirk?"

"What? Why?"

"Well, you know, following someone on social media is like following a story. I just want to make sure I'm telling an interesting story to my followers."

Dirk's brow crinkled. "What does that even mean?" he asked.

Marianne snorted. "It means he wants you out of the picture so it looks like he and Leigh have picked up two girls while in Panama. Am I right, Andy?"

Andy nodded. "I wasn't going to say it. Just, you know, leave it there and imply it."

"Not happening," Marianne said and sat back down, "just post the picture you have and let's get going."

Andy decided against forcing the issue and started punching in his message to go with the photo.

When they were ready and seated, Jorge started the engine. It was a rope start engine, and it took three attempts before spitting to life. Upon starting, it belched black smoke before settling into a rhythm. Marianne again gave Dirk a look, and he again responded with a shrug.

Jorge unhooked the mooring rope and pushed away from the dock. Once clear, he manually lowered the engine into the water and shortly after, they were away.

Jorge turned the boat north, and soon they were motoring along with Colón Island on their left and Carenero Island on their right. Ahead, the water grew choppier as the protection from the islands dropped away and they rode into the open sea.

"Of course," Andy shouted over the whipping wind, "no one ever heard of Crab Island in the archipelago because it's not part of the archipelago. It's out in the fucking ocean."

The boat started hitting bigger waves and bouncing higher. Everyone looked around for something to hold onto, but there was nothing close by and they all ended up clutching the gunwales.

Leigh's stomach started to feel a little queasy from the constant up and down motion of the boat as it bounced along the waves. He had been queasy since first climbing aboard. There was something about Jorge, and his boat, that made Leigh uneasy. He looked up at Jorge. The bulbous purple scar that ran down his neck from behind his ear down past the collar of his shirt stood out menacingly. As he stared at it, he noticed for the first time that there were other smaller scars branching off from the thick, primary scar. It was as though the first scar had been the result of flesh tearing, rather than it being from a cut. He shivered as he pondered the scar's origin.

Yes, Leigh decided, there was definitely something off about Jorge. Could they really trust him? For all Leigh knew, he could be taking them out to a remote patch of ocean, only to pull a gun, kill them all and dump the bodies overboard for the fish. Jorge did not look remotely like a legitimate tour operator, and no one really knew where they were or who they were with…

Leigh admonished himself. He was letting his imagination get away from him and thinking dark thoughts. He had to stop.

He looked around the boat. Both Dirk and Marianne clung to the side grimly. Inge seemed more at home, and he was again taken by the sight of her. She had let her hair out, letting it whip behind her on the wind. Leigh wished there was some way of watching her without being obvious. But there was none, so he instead focused on the horizon.

Twenty minutes in the open sea, the engine sputtered and died. Jorge turned, his expression dark as those heavy eyebrows arched down angrily. He kicked the bags in the centre aside. Dirk was about to protest when Jorge pulled up a floorboard and handed it to him to hold. From below the deck Jorge pulled a toolbox and stepped over to the motor, pulling the cover away to start tinkering with it. He unscrewed components and blew on the parts as if he had magic breath, all the while mumbling in Spanish. Every second word seemed to be '*puta madre*'.

Twenty minutes passed with all five passengers waiting quietly for Jorge as he continued to tinker. Twice he reassembled the motor but it failed to start. Marianne and Inge stripped off their shirts to reveal their bikinis underneath and clambered over the windscreen of the boat to sunbake on the bow deck while they waited.

After a further ten minutes passed Andy got to his feet and began pacing the deck. Leigh offered to take a photo of the moment to preserve the memory and share with his followers, but a tight-lipped, humourless smile told him Andy was not in the mood for jokes.

A full hour passed before Jorge finally brought the motor sputtering back to life. The engine coughed, sending up spouts of inky smoke to smudge the skyline in protest, but it worked, and shortly after, the girls clambered back over and they were on their way.

Leigh was just settling back into the monotonous grind of riding the bumpy waves while the wind whipped around him when Andy called out. Leigh turned to see an enormous grin on his face. He pointed forwards, and Leigh squinted at the horizon for his first glimpse of the speck that was Crab Island.

They all looked on eagerly as the island came gradually into view. Jorge slowed the boat down and started weaving back and forth in elongated S-shaped curves as they got close. Leigh stared at the island, unable to keep his eyes of it as they approached. For some reason, he had an enormous sense of foreboding.

Perhaps it was the look of the island? From what he saw as they neared, there were no trees on the island. It struck him immediately as strange. Even an island as remote as this should have trees, he thought. The island was large enough. At least five acres on his first estimates. A sandy beach stretched along the coastline ahead. A rocky cliff towered behind it on one side, and atop the cliff stood what appeared to be the craggy ruins of an old building. In the cliff he spotted a cave.

The opposite end of the beach led to a grassy plain. The grass was short, as though someone had recently run a lawnmower across it. There was a large flat area, which sloped upwards to the ruins. From this angle, the island bore a triangular shape, like a right-angled triangle with the ruins sitting at the peak. And that was literally it. Beach, cave and ruins. There was little else to do or see on the island. He wondered what made this such an attraction. Then Leigh turned once more to stare at the ugly purple scar on the back of Jorge's neck, wondering once more if this whole thing was a con.

Jorge pulled the boat up to the shore and let the boat beach itself on the sand.

"*Isla Azul,*" he announced. He stood up, leaving the engine running, and commenced picking up the bags of camping gear and throwing them over the front and onto the sand. Leigh frowned, wondering why the sudden haste.

"*Isla Azul*?" Dirk asked, "*azul* means blue. This is the wrong island." He stood up and tried to get Jorge's attention, but Jorge was in too much of a hurry. "Excuse me," he tried but was ignored. He reached out and grabbed Jorge by the shoulder. Jorge turned sharply and looked Dirk fiercely in the eyes.

"*Qué?*" Jorge asked aggressively.

Dirk was momentarily taken aback, and stumbled with his weak knowledge of Spanish.

"Ah, *incorrecto isla. Nosotros queremos isla*.... Crab," he stuttered.

"*Isla Cangrejo,*" Andy cut in.

"*Si,*" Jorge replied, "*esta es la isla de los cangrejos*."

Jorge seemed to regard this as the end of the conversation, returning to the gear and hauling it into the beach.

"What did he say?" asked Leigh, lost by the Spanish and suddenly feeling uneasy.

Dirk frowned and scratched his neck.

"This place is called Blue Island," Dirk began, "but when I asked him, I think he said it is the island of the crabs."

Andy snorted and threw his legs over the side to drop into the water below. "Crab Island or island of the crabs, what difference does it make? It's just semantics. This is the right place. Now hand me my bag."

Leigh passed his bag over the side and watched Andy walk to the shore. He turned back to see Dirk and Marianne exchange a quick whispered conversation in Dutch. Inge gave him a half smile.

Jorge reached down and picked up Leigh's bag and threw it onto the shore where it landed on a green canvas bag and tumbled across the sand.

"Hey, easy mate," Leigh complained, "I got breakable gear in there."

"Come on you lot, out of the boat," Andy called from the shore.

Leigh stood. His gear was already off the boat so he might as well get out too. He put his foot on the gunwale in preparation to jump when he paused. He looked up across the island. The sense of foreboding washed over him once more. Something just did not feel right about the place, but he could not put his finger on what it was. He looked at Jorge. Two nights and he would return. Maybe it was Jorge that bothered him, not the island. His demeanour gave Leigh no reason to trust him. Could he really believe Jorge would return and pick them up?

"Come on for fuck's sake," Andy groaned.

Leigh took a deep breath and dropped into the water. The water was warm and the sand soft beneath his feet. Close to the island, the waves were little more than ripples. This would make a great beach for swimming and relaxing. Leigh was about to walk to the shore when Andy called.

"Whoah there. Leigh, take that slab off Jorge. I don't want him throwing the beer ashore like the other stuff."

Leigh rolled his eyes. Of course, we must look after the beer. He turned as Jorge lowered the slab of cans onto his shoulder before walking ashore himself.

Jorge reached for one of the last three bags on the boat when Dirk thrust an open palm out to stop him. The whispered conversation had grown in intensity between Dirk and Marianne.

"Come on," Andy complained once more, "you've come this far, don't puss out now."

Jorge was equally impatient, grabbing the straps of the bag. Dirk had to lean forward and push down on the bag to stop him lifting it.

"*Te vas ahora,*" Jorge said impatiently.

More sharp whispered words were exchanged between Dirk and Marianne and it appeared Marianne was winning out.

"Well, I'm going," Inge suddenly declared. She stood and climbed over the front of the boat to step gracefully from the bow onto the sand.

Marianne watched her go, her gaze almost venomous. She rolled her eyes then looked out over the island. Finally, she nodded. Dirk lifted his weight off the bag and Jorge was quick to haul it over the edge and onto the sand.

Dirk and Marianne jumped off the side into the water. Their feet were barely wet when Jorge began asking for a push away from the shore. Andy and Leigh obliged. Jorge revved the engine and motored off without so much as a wave goodbye.

"Well, he was in a hurry to leave," Inge noted.

"He probably has an appointment," Andy said, waving the comment away. "We were stuck for, what, an hour? He probably doesn't want to be late."

Marianne suddenly yelped, and in a flash of foaming white water fled for the shore.

"What happened?" Dirk asked as he followed behind.

"I think something bit me," she said. She reached the shore and looked down to note a small red mark on the back of her ankle.

Dirk looked about him in the crystal-clear waters but saw nothing.

Leigh continued to feel an odd sense of foreboding as he watched Jorge again weave his boat in long S-shaped loops away from the island.

"Andy, you did pay him just a deposit, right?" Leigh asked.

"No, I gave him the full cost upfront. That was the deal."

Leigh continued to watch Jorge. He finished his exaggerated curves and now sped off towards the horizon. Leigh frowned and wondered if he would see that dilapidated boat again.

7

The afternoon sun beat down hard on the group as they traipsed across the island with their packs, looking for the ideal spot to hitch up their tents. In the centre of the island, they found a flat patch of ground that held a black smudge at the centre. From the look of the scuffed-up ground around it, this seemed to be a well-used campsite on the island.

Marianne gratefully dropped her pack as she glanced across their faces with one eyebrow raised. The silent, but unanimous vote, seemed to indicate that this, too, would be their camping spot.

Marianne sat on her bag and examined her foot. Whatever had bitten her had broken the skin slightly, and a small amount of blood had begun welling in the abrasion.

"Let's go get the rest of the gear," Dirk announced.

"You go along," Marianne said, "I just want to put some ointment on my foot, I'll be right with you."

Marianne dug through her pack and found her first aid kit. She broke the Velcro strapping and dug inside for the disinfectant ointment. It was a simple first aid kit, small, with bandages and scissors and strapping enough for any small injuries caused by cuts or scrapes, but nothing significant enough for anything major such as broken bones or cuts that required stitching.

It was only after she packed the first aid kit back away and turned to join the others did she notice she was not alone. Andy had stayed behind and was checking on his equipment in his bag. He looked up when she stood and gave her half a smile.

"You must be happy you've found the end of your quest," she jested.

"Yeah, I suppose," Andy said. He turned back to his gear and started re-packing his bag.

"That didn't sound too convincing," she replied.

"Oh, don't get me wrong, I am happy to be here, it's just…" his voice trailed off and he lifted his head and looked around. "It's just there's nothing here. I reckon we're on the least photogenic island in the entire Caribbean. I'm not sure it will go as well as I hoped on social media."

"What happened to this being all about the unique experience or whatever you said to sell it?"

He turned to her with an eyebrow raised. He clearly did not expect her to be so feisty.

"Oh, of course it is about that, but it also has to look good on social media. I'll have to find a way to dial up the viewability. Nobody goes to a person's page to see plain and boring pictures of empty plains and piles of dull rocks. What would be the point?"

Marianne shrugged. Internet fame and giving thousands of strangers a window into her life was never something that appealed to her. She was not what you would call an introvert, she just did not see her life as anybody's business other than her own and those who were close to her. Sometimes she felt like an alien amongst her friends, who were hooked onto social media like a drug, always taking photos of their food and selfies wherever they went. But she always felt it was born from a need to feel interesting rather than actually being so. Well, that's how she saw it, and Andy's obsession with the perfect photo was only enhancing that view. Besides, did people really want to see her life? She never stayed out late. She never broke laws or took drugs. She would take a night in front of the television snuggling with Dirk over a big night out ninety-nine times out of a hundred. She was boring. But more importantly, she was happy being boring, because she was content with the life she had and she never felt the need to flaunt it.

"If you say so," she responded. "Shall we go help the others?"

He nodded and stood up to fall in line with her as she walked.

There was a bit of an awkward silence as they walked. In the couple of days since they had met, they had barely spoken a word with each other. Andy made a couple of banal attempts to start a conversation which ended with a simple yes or no answer. And then he said something that really drew her attention.

"So, tell me about Inge," he started, "is she single?"

A surge of excitement ran through Marianne and she had to fight down the urge to smile. She had only come on this trip for Dirk and Inge. Dirk, so he had something to brag to his mates about, and Inge so she could have a holiday fling and get Martin out of her system. Marianne knew Inge still held a flame for Martin, that cheating piece of shit, and if Inge did not get him out of her system, she would probably let him back into her life when they returned home. As a friend, Marianne could not let that happen. She had already seen that bastard cause Inge enough heartache. She also wanted a bit of excitement, and while she was tied down and settled with Dirk, there was no reason she could not vicariously enjoy Inge's holiday affair with a handsome Australian guy.

"She just broke up with her boyfriend, so yes, she is single. Why do you ask?"

"Oh, just, you know," Andy answered uncommittedly.

I know exactly, Marianne thought as a smile crept over her lips.

Ahead they saw the others returning with the canvas bags that Jorge had rented them. Inside were tents, firewood and anything else they needed. Marianne suggested Inge looked like she was struggling with her bag and that Andy should take it from her.

"You wouldn't mind, would you?" Marianne asked. Butter would not melt in her mouth.

"Um, sure. No sweat," Andy replied. He jogged a few steps and offered to take the load off Inge's hands. She frowned, insisting it was not necessary, but then she caught a glimpse of Marianne's face and handed it over.

The boys walked on, leaving the two girls to walk back to the beach for the final bags.

"So, what was that about and why were you giving me that weird look just now?" Inge asked.

Marianne checked over her shoulder. She was bursting with excitement, and as soon as the boys were out of earshot she jumped in front of Inge and grabbed her by the shoulders.

"Guess what?" she asked, a maniacal grin on her face.

"Um… you've gone mad?"

"No, Andy!"

"Andy's gone mad?"

"No, Andy. He's into you."

Inge bit her lip to hold back from smiling.

"Really? How do you know?"

Marianne looked over Inge's shoulder, just to be certain the boys were a safe distance away.

"He was asking about you. He wanted to know if you were single. That's good, right?"

"I was kind of leaning towards Leigh. He seems like a nicer guy. He's, you know, less into himself."

"Pfffft Leigh. I think he's just being friendly. I haven't even seen him so much as flirt with you yet. Besides, Andy's cuter."

Inge stopped biting her lip and let the smile break free over her face. "He is, isn't he?" she giggled. "You really think he likes me?"

"Definitely. Listen, as we were walking back, I was thinking what you should do. You have to find a way to get Andy alone. Find a nice secluded romantic place on the island," Marianne paused for dramatic effect, "and then fuck him like a jackhammer."

They both burst out laughing, then quickly started shushing each other in case the boys heard.

Inge raised an eyebrow.

"And afterwards I suppose you want to hear all about it?"

"Every single detail." She laughed again, and they turned to walk down to the beach.

8

Setting up camp proved to be a greater toil than they had expected. The tents came with no instructions and for the most part they all felt like they were trying to create an origami crane without ever having seen the final result.

At one point, Andy stopped to film the calamity, as if it were something that needed to be kept for prosperity. He doubted the video would be any good, though. Too many raised middle fingers at the camera and complaints from the others that he was not helping to make it entertaining.

Eventually they had two tents successfully raised and pegged into the ground. It was late in the afternoon, leaving enough daylight for a good swim on the beach. Everyone was dripping with sweat and needed the cool off.

While Leigh was changing inside his tent, Andy pulled a couple of beer cans out, passing one to each of the girls and to Dirk. Dirk opened it and started downing it quickly.

"Ah," he exclaimed, "after hard work like that, this beer is like an angel pissing on your tongue."

Andy almost spat his beer out. "What?"

Dirk smiled. "It's an old Dutch saying. It means it tastes good."

Andy looked at him doubtfully. He took another mouthful of the warm brew. "I agree this beer tastes a bit like warm piss, but you've lost me on the angel bit."

"What's this about angel's piss?" Leigh asked as he emerged from his tent.

"Never mind," said Andy, reaching back into the groceries to pull another can for Leigh.

They walked slowly to the beach, warm beers in hand and towels draped over their shoulders. Leigh looked about the island, again fighting down the odd feeling that there was something not right about the place.

"Pretty boring, isn't it?" Andy asked.

"Boring?"

"Yeah, nothing about it to really light up my account."

Leigh frowned. Andy always seemed to have a one-track mind.

"It's not that," Leigh said, "it's just that there's something strange about the place."

"It's the lack of trees," Inge added, "or any wildlife. Plus, that ruined old building at the top of the cliff. It makes the whole place seem so desolate."

"I'm more worried about the lack of shade," added Dirk. "We're going to need a lot of sunscreen to get by without being burnt to a crisp. I'm worried my body will absorb so much of it that I'll be shitting sunscreen for the next three weeks."

"You apply too much screen anyway," Inge complained.

"Well, I need it. Can't you see my moles?"

Leigh smiled, enjoying the friendly banter. He took another sip of warm beer and looked about again. Perhaps Inge was right. Perhaps it was a feeling of desolation that was causing him to feel this way. They had just come from an archipelago of islands that teemed with life. Lush green plants bursting with colourful flowers. Trees alive with flapping birds, dozing sloths and swinging monkeys. The air filled with chirps, squeaks and the buzzing of insects. Even Bocas Town was lively with its vibrant colours, upbeat music and exotic food scents. Here there was nothing. No life. No colour. No smell. This island was quite the contrasting sensory shift.

They laid their towels on the beach and began applying sunscreen. Inge jovially teased Dirk over how much he was applying, jesting that at the rate he was going, they would run out of sunscreen by noon tomorrow.

Inge was first to approach the water, not waiting for Marianne to finish applying sunscreen to Dirk's back. Leigh watched her, trying not to stare too obviously at her curves. As she reached the waterline, she stopped and looked up and down the shoreline. She turned back to everyone with her face scrunched in confusion.

"Isn't this the place we got off the boat?" she asked.

"Yeah," answered Andy, "why?"

"It's weird. I don't remember the water being filled with rocks."

"It wasn't," Andy replied. "It was clean white sand as far as I could see."

"That's why it's weird. Because it's full of rocks now."

Everyone stopped and turned to look at her strangely.

"Don't look at me like that, come and see for yourselves."

Leigh sipped his beer and walked over to stand beside her. He looked into the water and saw hundreds of grey circular shapes through the sun-glinted ripples of the sea. They were oddly symmetrical and seemed half buried in the sand. It was difficult to judge the size properly due to the distortion created by the water, but he estimated they sized between six inches to a foot in diameter. The surfaces of the rocks were oddly smooth.

He looked left and right along the beach. Everywhere he looked the water was filled with the same shapes.

"What the fuck?" Andy said as he joined them, peering into the water.

Leigh bent down by the water's edge to get a closer look. He tried focusing on one rock. It was difficult to get a clear image through the rippling water. A small puff of sand rose from the front of the rock, and as Leigh focused, he was sure he could make out two small stalks protruding from the front of it. He stood up.

"They're crabs," he announced.

"What?" Marianne asked.

"They're not rocks. They are crabs."

Dirk joined them now to take in the phenomenon. He started walking up the beach, but there were grey shapes in the water as far as he could see.

"God," he exclaimed, "I can't see the end of them. There must be thousands of them."

"Aw shit," Andy exclaimed, "this must be the big attraction. I have to get my camera."

No one bothered to turn and watch him run back to the camp. They were all transfixed by the countless shapes in the water.

"Well, there's no way I'm going in there," Marianne stated.

"I agree," added Dirk. "Swimming is off for the time being. Maybe it was one of these that nipped you on the foot earlier. But where did all the others suddenly come from?"

"I think crabs come inland at night," Leigh said. "I remember seeing a documentary one time. They keep cool in the water or underground during the day and then roam around land at night." He turned to see the sun now getting low in the sky. "It's getting late, perhaps they are preparing to come ashore."

"Wait," said Marianne, her voice suddenly carrying an edge to it, "are you suggesting that all of those crabs are coming ashore?"

"Maybe."

Marianne's eyes widened as she turned back to the water. She shivered animatedly, as though the chill that ran up her spine did so with great violence. It might have looked comical, had the situation not felt so serious.

Dirk gulped and took a step back. "That is why Jorge called it 'island of the crabs'. It's their home."

"That documentary," Inge said, "did it say why the crabs come ashore?"

Leigh thought on it a minute but said nothing. He did not want to say, because he did not like the answer. The desolate island, void of any life. The haste in which Jorge made to leave. The extremeness and danger of staying overnight on the island. It all made sense. Too much sense.

The crabs were coming ashore to eat.

9

The crabs began the inland march at dusk. Like the invading army at Normandy, they poured out of the water and up the sandy beach of the island in waves. It was an odd army, raised as they were on six spindly legs and walking sideways, leaving scores of dotted tracks in the sand behind them. Their movements were oddly mechanical, and sometimes they surged forwards in bursts. They were mostly blueish in colour, and as per Leigh's original estimate, were a bit over six inches in diameter.

Andy was in his element, running about the beach with his camera, capturing the horde crawling inland from every possible angle, ordering Leigh to take certain shots of Andy with the waves of crabs. On many occasions Leigh wanted to roll his eyes, but Andy had lived every day since they arrived in Panama for this moment, so he did not complain.

The crabs, whenever Leigh or Andy strayed too close, would stand to their full height and raise their claws threateningly. In one moment of lapsed concentration, one crab latched onto Andy's thong and had to be shaken vigorously off.

"Aggressive little buggers," he said.

The swarm of crabs creeping onto the island seemed endless, and Leigh and Andy found themselves quickly becoming surrounded. Crabs were crawling over each other, their claws snapping at the air and their eye stalks waving about. Leigh noticed some of the crabs had dimorphic claws, meaning one claw being significantly larger than the other. In some instances, the bigger claw was as big as, if not bigger, than the carapace of the crab itself. Leigh took note not to stray too close to these ones in particular as they would no doubt deliver quite a nasty nip.

"Come on Andy, have we got enough yet?"

"No, just a couple more and then we'll go back and join the others."

Leigh looked down and saw the crabs were now crawling close to his feet. One, in particular, seemed to be eyeing him off, its black, orb-like eyes sitting up on their stalks examining him with intent. It was a big one too, almost a foot in diameter with an equally large claw. Leigh stepped up onto a rock to get out of its range.

Andy posed for a few more photos. He had barely wiped the wild grin from his face since the first sighting, but as the last photo was taken, he looked around once more and suddenly sobered.

"Jesus, there are a lot of these buggers."

He started gingerly walking between them, placing his feet with care wherever a gap existed.

Leigh looked down. The rock he stood on was completely surrounded now. The swarms of crabs were flowing around it like a flood of water. They crawled over one another, their spindly legs clicking as they passed over the carapaces of other crabs.

"What are you waiting for?" Andy called. "Let's get moving."

"There's nowhere for me to stand."

"Just walk on them then. I'm sure their species will survive a couple of deaths."

"I'm only wearing thongs."

Andy waved him away. "Just do it, you pussy. Otherwise, you're going to be stuck there all night."

Leigh looked down at the surging masses. There was no space at all, he would have to stand on them as Andy had said. He looked at the crabs closest to the rock and realised they were using each other to create a ladder. They were climbing over one another to reach him!

He saw the one with the big claw again. It was still, watching him with the same baleful eyes.

Leigh took a deep breath and committed. He leapt off the rock and ran across the sea of crabs. They crunched underfoot, and he moved quickly to avoid retaliation. Suddenly there was a sharp pain in his calf. He looked down to see a large crab had latched on with one claw and clung on despite the buffeting it received as he ran. As Leigh neared the edge of the wave, it squeezed tighter on his calf. His foot hit something, and suddenly he was staggering. Momentum carried him forward, but he could not regain himself and fell forwards onto the ground.

As Leigh looked up, a crab was mere inches from his face. It reared up aggressively, its claws raised warlike right before his eyes. For a moment Leigh stared the crab down, scared that any move would incite the crab to snip at his eyes. Then a foot pressed down on its back, holding it to the ground.

"Get up, and careful with my camera, mate."

Leigh pulled himself up and brushed down his shirt. The crab that latched onto his calf remained in place, and blood had begun trickling from the two points where the claws pierced the skin. They took a few steps away, but for now the crab horde stood motionless, their orb-like eyes watching every move.

Andy bent down and tried opening the claw that held Leigh tight. Leigh grimaced as the claw seemed to squeeze even tighter.

"Jesus," he complained, "this is one strong little bugger. I can't open his claw. Just a second."

Andy moved about the grass a second, before bending over to pick up two large rocks. He walked back to Leigh and bent down and readied himself to crush the crab by bringing the two rocks rapidly together with the crab in the middle. Suddenly, the crab let go and dropped back to the ground and scurried away.

They watched it go and then shared a glance but said nothing.

The ill feeling of dread washed over Leigh once more. These were not just ordinary crabs, there was something smart about them too. Just what kind of hellish place was this?

10

Darkness fell like a cloak across the island with a startling pace and the group were soon huddled around a small fire.

The flames greedily devoured the supply of firewood they had found amongst the camping gear Jorge had provided as the campers settled down. While Leigh and Andy were out taking photos, Dirk and the girls had started the small fire and set up a small wall around it with their backpacks. The wall was flanked on either side by the entrances to the tents. Over the fire, a pan sizzled as sausages fried noisily and beside it a potato filled pot bubbled noisily.

The group sat in silence. Marianne had wrapped Leigh's leg with a bandage from her kit, though it gave little relief from the pain and he constantly itched at it. Inge turned the sausages every few seconds, while Dirk stared blankly into the fire. Marianne cut up a small salad while every other second peering off into the darkness around them. She had the same taut muscled look she had when they were at the Nivida caves. Only Andy seemed content, his face lit up by the small screen of his camera as he browsed through the day's photos.

The food was served and plates were passed around. Andy opened another can and sipped the warm brew inside.

"We need to find a place to cool the beers," he said before belching loudly.

"Not just the beers. If we leave this food in the open sun it will be rotten before midday tomorrow," Inge pointed out.

"If the food went off, we could always eat crabs," Andy joked.

"What about the cave? It's probably cooler in there," Dirk suggested.

"As long as it's not crawling with crabs it should be ok."

"Can we not constantly talk about the crabs?" Marianne asked irritably.

Everyone went silent then. Ever since the first spotting, Marianne had been irritable. She had growled at Inge for putting too much water in the pot for the potatoes. It was she who had requested the bags be set up to form a barrier around the camp. She then had not liked the way Dirk had arranged the bag wall and ordered him to redo it all. She was clearly on edge.

The food was served and everyone started on their meals in silence. As Leigh chewed through his food, he started to become aware of an odd noise. He was not sure if he was imagining it at first, but the longer it went on, the more he started to believe he really was hearing it. It was a strange noise, like the ticking of a thousand clocks.

"Can anyone else hear that?" he asked.

"Hear what?" Andy asked.

"The ticking."

Everyone stopped chewing to listen. Dirk tilted his head to the side and frowned.

"What is that?"

Leigh put his plate to the side and stood up. He walked to the bag barrier and looked out. The ground ahead of him seemed to shift and heave as though it were alive. The quarter moon shone down, and low light only served to create a pit of shifting shadows. Leigh frowned.

"Can someone pass me a torch?" he called.

Dirk came up beside him with a torch in hand and flicked it on. All around them swarmed the crabs, their chitinous shells glowing dully and their oval eyes glinting in the torchlight. Their numbers were incredible, and everywhere they teemed over each other in a flood of shells, legs and claws. The ticking sound was that of legs on carapaces and the snapping of claws. Dirk took a step back as he shone the torch left to right, and then out into the distance. There seemed to be no end to their crawling ranks.

"Holy shit," Andy laughed, "there's millions of the buggers."

Leigh and Dirk worked their way around the barrier, shining the torch on their surroundings. Everywhere they looked they saw endless ranks of crawling, bug-eyed crabs.

"We're completely surrounded," Dirk said flatly.

"What?" asked Marianne in a nervous voice.

"The crabs. They're all around us for as far as I can see."

Marianne bit her lip and stared anxiously about. "Everywhere?"

Dirk nodded solemnly. Behind him, Andy started filming and narrating the scene. His voice was alive with excitement. Inge and Marianne stood up to look, but less than a second later Marianne sat back down and clutched her arms tightly about her.

"This is crazy," Inge said. "I see now why this place has such a legend about it. It's every bit, if not more, as crazy as going to Chernobyl."

"Andy was right," said Dirk, "this is something I'll be talking about for years. No one will have a story like it." Then Dirk, too, retrieved his phone and camera from his pack and started taking pictures.

Marianne clung to herself, eyes darting about her.

Leigh sat down by the fire and rubbed his calf where the crab had earlier clung onto him. Like Marianne, he did not see the thrill in this. This was not fun or exciting, this was creepy and scary. There were thousands, if not millions, of snapping crabs out there. What if they were all as aggressive as the one that attacked him earlier? And what if, as he had thought earlier, they had come ashore to feed? There was nothing here. If this is where they ate, and there was nothing here, they must be ravenous. And if there was nothing on the island for a ravenous horde and five people sitting around a fire then…

An image came into his head and he tried desperately to strike the thought from his mind. He did not want to think of the chitinous hordes swarming over the barriers, coming in droves to climb over them, dragging them down under the weight of their numbers and pulling them apart with their claws while they were buried under an avalanche of crabs. He shivered violently and shook his head, but the vision of crabs crawling over him was too vivid.

Suddenly Marianne screamed, breaking him from his thoughts. A crab had broken through the barriers and was stealing a sausage from one of the plates. It had one large and one small claw.

"Pick it up from behind," Andy said usefully, "thumb on the top and index and middle finger on the bottom."

"I'm not touching it," she screeched. "Get it away from me."

Dirk reached forward but the crab quickly turned, raising itself high on its legs and snapping its claws aggressively at him. Dirk moved his hand to the right. The crab made a quick scuttling manoeuvre to keep him in front. He moved his hand to the left; again the crab followed him, its oval eyes glinting in the firelight. But the little monster was so focused on Dirk it failed to see Inge approach behind it, scooping it up as Andy had said.

The crab reacted wildly, its legs and claws waving about erratically as it attempted to latch onto Inge. She panicked, and threw the crab out over the bags back into the clambering hordes.

Dirk kneeled beside Marianne and started to put his arm around her.

"Don't touch me," she screeched. She took a deep breath. "Sorry," she said in a more controlled voice, "I just don't want anybody or anything touching me right now."

"Ok," Dirk said and settled down to sit beside her without touching her.

Inge sat shortly after and retrieved her plate and continued to eat. Leigh stared at her blankly a moment before retrieving his own plate. He bit into a potato. It suddenly seemed bland and tasteless to him.

Andy was last to sit down, picking up a sausage with his fingers and taking a big bite. "This is amazing," he said, "these pictures and videos are going to send my social account into orbit."

Marianne glared at him.

"Jesus, Andy," Leigh swore, "try reading the room for once in your life."

Only then did Andy look up and see the sombre mood around him. He gave them all a weak smile and silently sat down with them.

They sat in silence for the rest of the meal. The ticking went on around them unabated. They piled the dirty dishes near the fire. Nobody was interested in cleaning them tonight. The silence in the group dragged on, and it was Marianne who finally broke it.

"I need to go to the toilet," she announced.

Leigh looked up and then around. He started to imagine the claustrophobia she must have felt. There was nowhere to go. They were trapped within their own wall of bags, guarded from escaping by thousands of warden crabs.

"You could pee in a pot," Inge suggested.

"It's… not that," Marianne replied.

Inge frowned for a second, then made her mouth the shape of an 'o'.

"Then shit in a pot," Andy said callously. "We can wash it out tomorrow."

Marianne looked at him sadly, and Leigh thought he may have seen a tear in her eye reflected by the firelight.

"OK," she said softly, "do you mind going into your tents? Dirk, I want you to stay with me."

Leigh nodded and stood. He unzipped the tent he and Andy would share and shone his light inside, searching the corners and blankets for movement before stepping inside.

The tent sat mostly outside the ring of backpacks, and all across the sides and rear walls of the tent, crab claws and legs scratched against the canvas. It was a soft sound, but to Leigh it was every bit as hideous as someone drawing their fingernails across a chalkboard.

"Can you believe that?" Andy asked when the tent was closed behind him. Leigh glared at him and Andy rolled his eyes. "Women."

Leigh turned away and shook his head.

"This place is amazing," Andy continued. He sucked in a deep breath and held it, as though he was tasting and preserving the memory of the air around him. "This is even more amazing than I thought it would be."

"Amazing? Are you kidding?" Leigh spat. "This isn't amazing, this is terrifying."

"What? Terrifying? They're just crabs, mate."

Leigh shook his head. Andy just could not see it. They were prisoners here. They only had a small area to move within and beyond that, hordes of snippy creepy crawly crabs. They were trapped, so much so that only a few feet away behind a thin canvas tent flap Leigh could hear Marianne grunt as she defecated into a cooking pot because there was literally nowhere to go.

And then, in the morning, if the crabs went back into the ocean, they would still be trapped here on the island, only to go through the whole experience again tomorrow night.

Leigh was thinking of having to spend another night like this and watching a crab claw silhouette drag down the canvas when Andy tapped him on the arm and leaned forward conspiratorially.

"Hey, have you made a move on Inge yet?"

"Huh?" Leigh was thrown by the sudden change in topic. He shook his head. "No"

Andy licked his lips. "Well, I was talking to Marianne and it turns out that young Inge only just broke up with her boyfriend." Andy smiled and waggled his eyebrows up and down suggestively.

"What? How is that important information?"

"Because she'll be looking for a rebound fuck, mate. You can be that rebound fuck."

"Andy, I don't think this is the right setting…"

"Jesus, Leigh, you always have an excuse not to make a move. What are you so afraid of? Nobody cares about setting. Remember when I fucked that girl in a portable toilet at that music festival? Do you think she cared about setting?"

Leigh rolled his eyes in response.

"Look, Leigh, stop making excuses and just do it. Grab the bull by the horns. Or, as it is in this case, grab the girl by the hips."

Leigh let out a sigh. Making a move on Inge was the last thing he wanted to think about right now. He was too distracted by the endless ticking that filled the air, the silhouetted claws raking against the tent canvas in front of him and the thousands upon thousands of crabs that surrounded their fragile little camp, who could at any moment pour over the breach. The vivid thought of them climbing all over him and snipping him with their claws would not go away. He shuddered. No, making a move on Inge was not something he wanted to talk or think about right now.

"We're done," Dirk called from outside the tent. Leigh got up and exited the tent without saying a word.

Outside, the constant ticking was louder, but the release from the scratching and scraping of claw on canvas did give

Leigh some relief. Marianne again clung to herself, looking smaller than Leigh remembered her to be. She looked like a frightened child.

Inge clambered out of her tent opposite, giving Leigh a half smile. She knelt down beside Marianne and they had a short, quiet exchange in Dutch.

"My turn," Andy announced, and stood up on the backpack wall. He unzipped himself and started peeing over the crabs on the other side. He laughed. "You want some of this, you little buggers?" he taunted them. After a quick shake he fixed his pants, got down and turned to see the shocked faces of the others. "What?"

"Marianne is worried about them coming inside," Dirk said, "I don't think antagonising them is a good idea."

Andy rolled his eyes. "They're just dumb crabs. Why are you acting so weird about them?"

"They're horrible," Marianne said, her voice uncontrolled. "They're all creepy and crawly, like spiders with claws. Only bigger."

"And you saw what that one did to my leg," Leigh added, "now imagine them coming over the bags a hundred at a time and clamping onto us like that."

Marianne looked at Leigh with horror in her eyes. "Oh god, I didn't even think of that."

"They are not going to come over the bags, guys," Andy said, "relax." But one look at Marianne and Leigh's faces let him know they were not convinced. He approached the fire and pulled a burning piece of wood from it. He walked back to the bags, then nodded his head for the others to join him.

Marianne glanced at Dirk, who nodded in assurance. She slowly got up and walked towards Andy with trepidation. Leigh and the others followed.

"Right," Andy said, "watch this."

He dropped the burning wood a couple of feet outside the small ring they occupied. Almost immediately there was a flurry of activity as the crabs reacted as the wood landed amongst them. Legs clacked against shells and claws waved aggressively at other crabs as they fought each other to get away from the burning embers. After a few moments of panicked activity, a small hole in their ranks had opened with the burning torch on the ground. The small circle had formed around the crabs, and their oval eyes glared at it balefully.

"See," Andy pronounced victoriously, "they hate the fire. If any brave the inner circle, we can drive them away with fire."

"But that would mean staying up all night," Marianne said.

"We could do it in shifts," Dirk suggested.

"I'm not sitting out here alone with… them," Marianne said, waving her hand in the direction of the clicking horde.

"Nobody who is unwilling to will be forced to," Andy announced. "I take it you're fine to do one shift, Dirk?"

Dirk nodded.

"Great, what about you, princess?"

Leigh was staring at the ring of crabs around the burning wood. As the flame sputtered, they inched ever closer. There was a moment of silence, and Leigh only then realised Andy had been talking to him. He looked up and met Andy's eye. He then looked at Inge and realised she was watching him intently.

"Yeah, I'll do a shift," he said, cursing his pride.

11

It was a little after midnight that Leigh crawled alone into his tent. He shined the torch around, checking the canvas walls for any cuts or tears. All seemed intact and in order. Next, he checked the tent for movement, before finally patting down on all the bedding. He did not want any unwanted guests or surprises as he tried to sleep. Satisfied the tent was crustacean free, he settled to sit on his bed. He rolled his muscular shoulders, trying to ease the tension from them.

Andy was taking the first shift, and would come to wake him in a couple of hours. Two hours would not provide a restful sleep, but Leigh could not have backed out. Not in front of Inge.

Leigh lay down on his bedding and closed his eyes in an attempt to sleep. It was stuffy inside the tent. The crabs, as before, were all around the tent walls. The scratching of claw on canvas and ticking of chitinous feet on carapace shell was ever present. Leigh turned to one side, then seconds later tuned to the other. The layer of bedding was thin, and the ground was rock hard underneath. He may as well have been sleeping on a stone bed at the side of a volcano.

Leigh sighed and turned over again. He lay a moment with his eyes clenched shut. He sat up and pulled off his t-shirt and lay once more, this time on his back. The scraping of claw on canvas was all around him, driving into his brain like hammered nails. He turned onto his side. It was no use. The two hours would be over and he would not have slept.

He opened his eyes and stared at the canvas walls of the tent. He could make out the shapes of the various individual crabs, their bodies pressed against the canvas while their claws banged or scraped the material like an angry protester. He tried to imagine how Marianne was coping. Better than he was, he hoped.

He rolled onto his back and stared at the roof. He wondered how much alcohol they had brought with them. Tomorrow, he thought, he would take the first shift. That way he could drink himself silly and pass out when his turn was over rather than trying in vain to fall asleep like this again.

Leigh turned once more. It was no use. Even if he could get past the stifling heat of the tent, the hellish noise was ever persistent in his head. It did not matter what he tried thinking about, the noise always brought him back to the nightmare present and the hordes of crabs that crawled and climbed on the other side of the thin canvas walls of the tent. And with the memory of the crabs, and their numbers, came the dreaded thought of them climbing past the barriers and crawling all over him. No matter what, he could not shake that horrible idea from his head.

Then Leigh sat up. He had a thought. He dug through his pockets and found his phone and headphones. He had switched his phone off not long after arriving. There was no use for it. There was no signal out here. But he could still listen to the stored music and block the horrid sound out.

He switched it on and plugged his headphones in. The time came up. Forty-five minutes had already passed. Had he really been tossing and turning that long?

He selected an album to listen to and laid back down. He was old fashioned in the way he consumed music. He liked listening to full albums, not playlists. His music taste, and the way he listened to music, was heavily influenced by his father. He would much rather sit back and listen to a full progressive rock album in its entirety than jump through a playlist of hot hits. Which is what he did now.

He closed his eyes and let the music wash over him. He wanted the music to absorb him. He wanted the notes, the lyrics, the winding melodies, all of it to wrap themselves around him and take him on a journey. He wanted the music to carry him away from this horrible place. He concentrated on the music, riding the ups and downs that even after listening to a hundred times still came across as fresh. But every silent space between tracks it was there. The ever-present sound of the crabs was just not going away.

The album finished and he was still awake. He opened his phone. Only half an hour until his shift. He decided to listen to another album. There was no use in trying to sleep now. He picked something a little more upbeat.

He closed his eyes again and this time started thinking about Inge. Should he make a move, here on the island, just as Andy had suggested? Maybe he could ask her to have a walk with him alone. He could see how she was coping, get her to open up to him, maybe get the chance to put his arm around her and comfort her. That would be the start of it. She would turn to him for support and strength, and he would be her man. Her protector.

It would be different this time, he knew it. Different than what had happened with Angela, or Carly, or any of the others. This time it was real, and he had a keyring that proved it.

He imagined the scene in his head, playing it over and over in his mind. He was so much cooler in his imagination. He always came up with the best lines. He set the scene on the beach. A beach was the perfect setting. Beaches were always romantic. He played the scene over, the two of them walking down the beach together. She was dressed in a tiny bikini and constantly admiring his broad shoulder muscles. It was a beautiful scene.

It was the fourth or fifth time he imagined walking down the beach with Inge when Leigh drifted finally off to sleep.

12

It was the heat that woke Leigh up. He was sweating profusely, and he had been tossing and turning when it finally got the better of him.

He slowly came to consciousness. His ears ached, and he realised his headphones were still in them. He tried remembering the night before. He could not remember listening past the second or third song of the album.

He pulled the earphones out and opened his eyes. It was daytime. His mind was still foggy, but something nagged at his brain that something was off. He turned over and saw the inert body of Andy lying next to him in the tent.

Andy! Shit!

He sat up, alertness coming to him with a rush. He looked around. There was silence, and there were no silhouettes of crab bodies or claws against the canvas of the tent.

Leigh turned back to his sleeping friend. Had he stayed awake all night until the crabs left?

Leigh wiped his brow with the back of his hand. Outside the tent he heard Dirk's voice. He was speaking Dutch. Marianne answered him. Her voice was still tense. Leigh decided to go out and see what was happening.

His bedding was a mess from all the tossing and turning, so he quickly made it up. He frowned at the wet patch on his pillow. He sure had sweat a lot during the night. He dared a quick sniff of his armpit and recoiled quickly. He stank. He looked around the tent for his deodorant and realised he had left it in his backpack outside. He had no choice. He would have to go out stinking like an unwashed animal. He pulled on his t-shirt and went outside.

As he exited the tent, Leigh was confronted by three hostile stares. The campsite was a mess. The ground was strewn with rubbish; torn packaging, broken eggshells, scraps of paper and plastic lay on the ground as though a bin had been upended and the garbage tossed around them. Each of the Dutch trio held bags in their hands and had been cleaning up the mess when he had emerged. The fire in the centre of the camp was cold, with not even a wisp of smoke rising from the ashes.

"What happened out here?" Leigh asked as he stood up.

"We were waiting for you to come out of the tent so we could ask you the same thing," Marianne replied.

"Me? I don't know anything about this."

All three stared at him a moment. Then Dirk asked something in Dutch. Inge replied. Leigh suddenly felt like he was on trial. He could feel the sharpness of their gazes cutting his flesh.

"Why didn't you wake me at the end of your watch?" Dirk asked, though his tone made it come out as an accusation.

"I… I never went on watch. Andy never woke me."

"That's a lie," Inge spat venomously.

Leigh turned to her now and realised of all three, she was staring at him the most hatefully. He suddenly felt sick. What had Andy done last night? He tried to remember the time when he last checked his phone before dazing off. It was just before two. He was sure of it. Andy had to be at fault.

"Andy must have stayed out longer and… I don't know."

Inge threw her bag on the ground. "This is bullshit," she yelled. She stepped over the backpacks and started storming off. She had taken a few strides when she stopped and turned. "He should clean it all up, not us." She turned and continued to stride away.

Leigh watched her storm away, feeling his chances of being with her were suddenly disappearing. Then he thought about Andy, asleep in the tent. He was the cause of this mess. He would need to confess when he woke up. He needed to clear Leigh's name so he could one again be in Inge's good graces.

Leigh turned back to Dirk and Marianne who watched him contemptuously.

"This is Andy's fault. He will clear it up when he wakes."

Dirk shook his head and turned away. Marianne continued to glare.

"You really need to stop lying. We know Andy went into the tent at two and woke you," Marianne said.

"What? No, he never came in at that time."

"Yes, he did."

Leigh shook his head. Why were they putting this all on him? He had done nothing and yet, here they were playing judge, jury and executioner and putting the whole mess on him.

"How would you know what time he came in?"

"Inge was with him."

The words hit him like freezing water thrown from a bucket. Inge was with Andy last night?

"What?"

Marianne smiled as though she had just played a winning move in a game of chess.

"Yes, she was up with him. She couldn't sleep, so she got up and chatted with him until two am, at which point she watched him go in and wake you up."

Leigh was shocked. He turned away, suddenly confused. Andy never woke him, did he? No, the last thing he could remember was lying there with his earphones in listening to music. There was a mistake. He wanted to wake Andy and quiz him. He looked back at the accusing face of Marianne.

"Look, I don't know what happened. I never woke up. I'm sure Andy can clear things up when he wakes up. In the meantime, why don't you sit down and I'll prepare some breakfast and then help clean up."

Dirk picked up a torn piece of packaging and stuffed it into a bag. He looked up scornfully.

"Make breakfast? With what? Grass and rocks? Eggshells and chocolate wrappers?"

Leigh frowned, then realisation hit him and he stared wide eyed at the mess about him. Torn packaging. Ripped boxes. Broken eggshells. No, surely not…

"What is going on?" he asked softly, already feeling he knew the answer.

"They ate everything."

"Ate everything?"

"Yes, those fucking crabs. They ate everything. Every single scrap of food is gone." Dirk dug into the bag he held and pulled out a yellow and red beer can. It had been torn open, its sides lacerated with tears and puncture marks. "They even destroyed all the beer."

"Do we at least have fresh water?"

"That's literally the only thing we have left."

Leigh's mind reeled. He remembered the crab that clung to his leg. How strong it held on while he ran despite all the buffeting but then dropped away when Andy picked up the two stones to crush it. These crabs were smart. They had surrounded them last night and waited. They had waited deliberately, and when the time came, they had scaled the walls and raided their food. They had been clever about it. These were no ordinary crabs.

The sound of a zip behind him broke Leigh from his reverie. Andy emerged, blinking.

"Do you lot have to talk so loudly?" he asked. He rubbed his eyes and as he pulled his balled fists away, he stared about wildly. "Shit, did you lot have a party without me?"

"We weren't on the invite list either," Dirk answered. "It was a crab party, and they ate everything."

Andy was still blinking. He was still waking up. "How did this happen?"

"You didn't wake me," Leigh cut in.

"Yeah, I did." Andy looked up to see Leigh frowning at him. "What? We talked for like a minute."

"No, you never…"

"Oh, give it a rest Leigh," Marianne cut in loudly. Her eyes were ablaze. "It's bad enough you let this happen, we're now without any food for the next day and a half, but not owning up to it is even worse. We thought you were a nice guy but this is some really low shit you're pulling right now."

Leigh bit his tongue to avoid responding. Could it be his fault? No, Andy had never woken him. But Andy said they had conversed. Maybe Leigh had talked in his sleep? That was possible, but the looks on everyone's faces in this moment make him realise it would be a mistake to suggest it. When you are in a hole, stop digging.

He dropped his head, and quietly joined the clean-up.

13

By mid-morning the site was cleared and bags of rubbish were piled against the backpacks and the campers all sat quietly entrenched in their own thoughts. Leigh's stomach ached from hunger. He looked at the morose faces of the others, wishing he had something to do or say that could get him back into their good graces.

"Is there any way we can get in touch with Jorge? Maybe he can pick us up a day earlier?" Dirk asked.

Andy shook his head sadly. "No. Even if one of us had a satellite phone, which we don't, we still don't have his number. No. He'll pick us up tomorrow as originally agreed. We just have to wait it out."

"And starve in the meantime?" Inge added.

"The human body can survive over eight days without food as long as we have water," Leigh said, but immediately regretted it. He looked down at the dirt in front of him, feeling their glares and not wanting to meet their gazes.

"I could catch and cook up some crabs," Andy suggested. "They ate our food, so now we eat them. I'd call that karma."

Marianne shivered. "Crabs. Why did you have to remind me of the crabs? I don't think I can go through another night like last night."

Andy sighed. "Look, I get you were creeped out by them and they ate all our food, but really, they are quite harmless."

"Are they? What happens if they come up on the island again like last night to feed and find no food. What then? Do they come for us?"

Leigh swallowed. He was not the only one who had had that thought then.

Andy was about to laugh, when he caught the glare in Dirk's eye and muffled it into a cough. Dirk then put his arm around Marianne and comforted her. "It's all right, they won't do that. They are scavengers. That's why they came for the food when no one was around."

Marianne nodded, but tears pooled in her eyes. She was biting her lip hard, and it looked like she was about to break the skin when she spoke. "But what about the big one?"

"Big one?" Andy asked.

Dirk rolled his eyes. "Marianne had a dream last night she saw a giant crab."

Marianne pushed his arm from around her. "It wasn't a dream," she said. She wiped her eyes and looked up earnestly. "I woke in the night and I saw its shadow over the tent. It was as big as a horse."

Andy frowned and held out his hand to stop her. "Wait, you only saw a shadow? Not the crab itself, just a shadow?"

"That's right."

"Well, it was probably a trick of the light. Crabs don't get that big. It was probably standing near the fire and its shadow was projected that way."

"No, you don't understand. The shadow was from above. It was a shadow from the moonlight."

Andy looked at her doubtfully, then shrugged. If that is what she wanted to believe, then that's what she would believe. It was probably, as Dirk suggested, just a dream. With crabs all around, plus her ingrained fear of animals, it would not be surprising that crabs would plague her thoughts and dreams as well.

"Ok, getting back to our current situation," Dirk jumped in, "we have no way of getting off the island. We can catch crabs for dinner but we'll have to go hungry until then. Thanks to Leigh, we have enough firewood to get us through another night, so we should be able to hold them off as long as everyone keeps their watch. We can get through this. It's no big drama."

His speech seemed more aimed at convincing Marianne than anything else, but Leigh imagined that a small part of it was convincing himself as well.

Andy stood up and dusted off his shorts. "Well I, for one, am not going to spend my day sitting here and moping about things that are not in my control. Dirk's right, we just have to ride it out, but that doesn't mean sitting around and staring at the ground." Andy opened the tent and reached in to withdraw his camera. He quickly checked the battery and nodded. "I'm going to check the ruins on the clifftop up there, if anyone wants to join me."

Without waiting, he stepped over the packs and started the uphill walk to the ruins. Leigh felt obliged to follow his friend, but held back. Andy was probably also disgruntled with Leigh over the incident, but he did not seem too outwardly fussed about it. In fact, he almost seemed to relish the idea that he now had an excuse to catch and eat crabs for dinner. In a few days, back in Bocas Town, they would be laughing about it over a beer and referring to themselves as the next Bear Grylls for having survived with no food.

But Inge, and the others, well that was a different matter altogether. Inge had not looked at him once since returning to the camp. Leigh ached to speak with her, to see her smile at one of his lame jokes, to restore that comradery they had found in recent days. Ever since he first saw her on the bus, he had been naturally drawn to her like a gravitational force. He realised, as he got to know her, that there was more to his attraction to her than just looks. She was incredibly easy for him to talk to. More so than any other woman he had met before. Their minds were alike, and he almost felt already he could finish her sentences for her. He had started to believe this was more than just a coincidence. She was unique. One of a kind. Something fate put in his path for a reason. They were meant to be.

And that was why he would not join Andy. He had to stay with Inge and her friends. He needed to get some time with her. Explain the misunderstanding. He must have talked in his sleep. He was convinced of it now. Andy had entered and he had talked in his sleep. He just needed to explain it. She would understand. She had to. They were meant to be together, he just needed to pass this hurdle. No relationship ever ran smoothly, the test of a good relationship was how couples got past their problems. He and Inge would get past this.

"He's right, we can't sit here all day," Dirk said.

Marianne looked at him. Her lips were pursed and there was still a wetness to her eyes, but she nodded. "I want to go to the beach. I want to make sure those things are gone and, if they are, I want to get in a swim before they return."

Dirk nodded and opened his backpack to retrieve a couple of towels.

Leigh saw his opening. Inge was likely to go with her friends to the beach, so he must as well. But if he waited for her to say it first, he would be like an awkward tag along, so he jumped in before she could speak up.

"I'll join you," Leigh said, jumping to his feet. Dirk and Marianne frowned, but he ignored them and opened his own pack to retrieve a towel.

"And you, Inge?" Marianne asked. "Will you join us?"

Inge pursed her lips. She met Marianne's eye, and there seemed to be an unspoken communication between them. Finally, she stood up. "No, I think I'll join Andy at the ruin. I'll catch you all later."

She turned and stepped over the packs, jogging a little to catch up to Andy. Leigh turned and watched her go. It was like a dagger to the heart. Did she hate him that much for what happened? Now he knew, more than ever, he had to clear the air with her.

"Are you coming?" Dirk shouted over his shoulder as he and Marianne walked towards the beach.

For a moment he considered changing his mind and chasing after Inge and Andy, but if things were already awkward with her, that would only make things worse. No, he would have to find another moment. He would have to leave it for now, following would only make things worse. He watched a little longer, her brightly coloured yellow and red striped t-shirt blowing gently in the breeze as she jogged.

Wistfully, he turned to follow Dirk and Marianne.

14

Andy was glad to get away from the others. He hated being around people who only wanted to whinge and complain. Yes, the situation was bad, but what good would sitting and moping actually do? He hated the grumbling more so because it was something that his generation was branded with. "*Oh, those millennials, they are all so self-entitled because they have grown up with the internet and always had everything at their fingertips. They would not know what hardship is, they are used to having everything and just complain when they do not.*" Argh. People who said that made him want to scream, and people of his own generation who behaved that way only wanted to make him scream even more, because all they did was prove the wretched stereotype to be true.

That was why he could not stand it. He was not a whinger. He was a doer. He worked to earn his privilege. He did not come by all those followers on social media by accident. He worked at it. He always challenged himself to create the most interesting and exciting content. To be someone worth following. To cultivate an audience. Yet how did older people see it?

"That's not a real job," his uncle would say. "When are you going to stop mucking around and taking photos of yourself and do something with your life?"

He just did not understand. Nobody from his generation ever would. But Andy would show them. He would earn a living and, if he worked hard enough, get rich doing it. He would show it off too. He would make sure they all knew. This did not happen because he was lazy, or entitled. It was not going to happen by fluke. It was going to happen because he worked hard, created great content, did his research and knew what his audience wanted to see. He was a new brand of entrepreneurs; one whose product was themselves.

Andy was walking briskly up the hill when he felt a tap on the shoulder. He turned to empty space and heard a giggle. He smiled wryly, certain that people had played that same old trick since the days of Christ. He looked over his other shoulder to see Inge grinning at him.

"Hey," she said coolly, "you need some company? I can take pictures of you if you want."

"Sure, I'd love the company."

She smiled wider and looped her arm through his as they walked. The closeness of the gesture caused their bodies to occasionally bump softly as they walked. Andy suddenly became aware of the close proximity and he looked at her properly for the first time. He had not paid too much attention to her before, largely due to Leigh's interest, but after last night's long chat by the fire and the looping of arms now, he started seeing her for the first time.

She was not supermodel hot or pedestal worthy, as she seemed to be to Leigh, but she certainly was what Andy would consider as 'above average'. She had wonderfully clear hazel-green eyes, and her face was pleasantly freckled. Her nose ring suited her, and gave her face an added layer of sexiness, a seemingly rebellious mark against her otherwise soft features. She had dimples on her cheeks, which added a layer of cuteness to her, especially when she smiled, which is what she was giving him right now.

He gave her a wink and turned back to the ruins.

He started thinking about last night at the fire. It had surprised him that she had decided to join him by the fire after everyone else had gone to bed. She had sat close, and had often touched his leg or arm when he joked. He considered at the time she may have been flirting, but had dismissed it. But now, with the linking arms as they walked, he was starting to become certain. She liked him.

He looked over his shoulder to see if anyone else was coming. He could see the distant forms of Leigh, Dirk and Marianne walking slowly to the beach.

So, he thought, some alone time with Inge and she seems to like me. He wondered if this had been arranged. He wondered if the others knew, and were leaving them be. He wondered, as well, if Leigh had seen this and accepted that she was not into him. Poor Leigh. He really did not know how to be with women. He spent all that time lifting weights, thinking muscles alone would attract women to him, but never changed his approach.

As they walked, Inge started chatting about her life back home in the Netherlands. Her manner was breezy and light, and Andy found it a refreshing change from the grim mood of the camp. He started to become glad she had joined him.

As they approached the top of the hill, Andy could see the ruins more clearly. The ruins appeared to be the remains of a black stone house of some sort. The shape was vaguely rectangular, with most of the first two layers of stonework remaining in place. At some points the ruins still stood as high as Andy's chest, but it was mostly only two stones high. The stones must have been imported as they resembled nothing they had seen on the island. The back-wall ruins sat right against the cliff, and leaning over it you could look down onto rocky outcrops and the sandy beach below.

"I wish there was some sort of plaque or something to tell us what this building was for, or who lived here," Andy said.

"Does it matter?"

"I suppose not. It would just make a better story when I post it, is all."

"Maybe you could search it on the internet when we get back?"

"Maybe, but I doubt it. It was hard enough just finding out whether or not this island was real to begin with. I'll ask Jorge. Maybe he knows."

Inge looked around, then out at sea. The glittering water stretched all the way to the horizon. "Maybe it was a lighthouse," Inge suggested.

"Maybe," Andy said. He stepped forward and held out his camera to her. "Do you mind doing the honours? I have some ideas for shots."

She reached out, and her hand brushed his as she took the camera. Their eyes met at the touch and lingered longer than necessary. He smiled, and backed away for the first shot.

He posed for a few videos. Normally at first, but after a small amount of teasing for his 'serious face', Andy started making silly poses such as muscle flexes and mock catalogue model pointing out to sea. Inge laughed as he posed, and the fun soon became infectious.

"Now take some pictures of me," Inge suggested, handing the camera back to Andy. Her first few poses were silly ones, her eyes wide and her tongue lolling out the side of her mouth. Then she changed to sexy poses, straddling rocks with her legs spread open or bending over a section of wall. After a few photos they reviewed what they had already taken. Inge leaned in close to view the small screen on the back of the camera, her soft breasts brushing against his arm.

"What do you think?" she asked as they viewed one of her provocative poses on the small screen.

"Hot," he said in reply.

"You really think that?" she asked innocently.

He turned and their eyes met. A gust of breeze blew her hair across her face and he moved it gently aside with his fingertips.

He was not sure who made the first move. Did he lean in and kiss her, or did she raise her head and kiss him? But as they kissed a second, third, fourth time, he realised that small detail did not really matter. For a second, Andy felt a tinge of guilt about kissing the girl that Leigh liked so much. But then he admonished himself. She was not interested in Leigh. She was interested in him. Whether or not Leigh saw her first was irrelevant, you cannot put dibs on girls.

Inge placed her hand on Andy's thigh and slowly started moving it gently towards his crotch. He realised then this was more than just a quick pash. He slid his hands down her back and slipped them under her t-shirt. She broke off the kiss and pulled the t-shirt over her head to reveal her bikini clad body underneath. She threw the t-shirt aside. It was caught by the wind and it blew, unbeknownst to the both of them, over the side of the cliff and snagged on a rocky outcrop below.

The two lovers continued to kiss as their hands explored each other's bodies, removing any and all clothing that hindered their journey. It was not long before they were both naked and enjoying the pleasure of flesh against flesh as they writhed on the ground in the ruins. They explored each other with their hands and then their tongues. And then he was inside her, thrusting energetically until his body spasmed with the pleasure of climax.

He rolled to the side and lay beside her. She turned and pressed slightly against him to continue that warm feeling of skin on skin. He looked her in the eyes and brushed her cheek with the back of his fingers as they kissed once more. Nothing could spoil this moment.

And that is when they heard the first scream from below.

15

Leigh dragged his feet and kicked the dirt as he followed behind Dirk and Marianne. This was not at all how he imagined the day to be. He should be the one alone with Inge, not Andy. She was meant to be his. But the incident with the food had obviously angered her. Why else would she skip the beach and go and look at a bunch of old rocks?

He looked over his shoulder back at her. She had almost caught up to Andy now as he walked up the hill towards the ruins. She appeared to be sneaking up on him. Good, he thought, give the bastard a fright, that was what he deserved for not owning the blame for the error in waking Leigh up.

Leigh turned away scowling. He wished Andy would take the blame. Admit he had not checked properly to make sure Leigh was awake, or at least admit he did not wake him so Inge would be angry with him and not Leigh. That is how Leigh saw things.

He imagined it was him, not Andy up in the ruins with Inge. He could finally make his move. 'Settings don't matter' Andy had said. Alone on the hilltop was a perfect location. They would reach the top and look out over the island and ocean. She would remark about how it was such a beautiful view. And then he would turn to her and look her smoulderingly in the eye and say "not as beautiful as the view I have of you". And then they would kiss. It was all so perfect. Damn Andy. He would have to convince him to own up to not waking him properly so he could take Inge up to the ruins later.

Ahead of him, Dirk and Marianne had set foot on the beach and began laying out their towels. Dirk took off his shirt and Marianne stripped off to her swimsuit. Dirk had brought the sunscreen and began applying it liberally to his chest while Marianne again teased him over how much he applied.

"I'm going to taste sunscreen every time I kiss you for the next month," she remarked.

Leigh walked past them, dropping his towel without laying it down properly. He wished he and Inge could be like them. Familiar, happy and in love. Marianne and Dirk seemed so good together. They were two parts of a whole, and could not be anything without their other half. Maybe he and Inge could be like that. It certainly felt that way when they talked. He could talk to her for hours and hours and never want to stop.

Leigh walked to the water's edge and stopped. He had been so wrapped up in his thoughts he had barely taken the time to look about him.

"How's the water?" Marianne called out.

Leigh blinked. He needed to stop fantasising, he told himself. Take a break, enjoy the beach for a moment. Inge can come later. He took in a deep breath and looked down into the crystal-clear water of the beach.

Crabs. Everywhere.

It was just like the evening prior. The water was full of them. They sat, half buried under sand, looking like rocks with their eye stalks the only indication they were anything else. He imagined they were looking back up at him. Their beady little oval eyes looking up through the gentle waves at him. What is it they saw when they looked at him?

"Well?" Marianne called again. "How does it look?"

Leigh bowed his head and turned. "It's full of crabs," he said.

"What?"

Marianne stormed over to the shore leaving a long streak of white sunscreen only half rubbed into her back by the bemused Dirk who stood dumbfounded for a moment before joining them. She stopped at the edge of the water and stared.

"Jesus," she swore under her breath.

Dirk approached from behind and put his hand out to continue rubbing the sunscreen in. She arched her back away from him at his touch, as though she had been touched by something cold and slimy.

"Don't touch me," she screeched. She turned and began pacing the beach. The sand kicked up and sprayed about under her hurried steps.

"Marianne…"

"No, just stop. You cannot understand what I am going through right now." Her face was twisted as though she were enduring physical torture. "This island, those crabs, it's all just so…ugh." She stopped a moment, back turned. Then she turned and again there were tears in her eyes. "Do you realise how stressful last night was for me knowing all those creepy crabs were all around us like that? Listening to them constantly scratching at the tent? They make my flesh crawl, Dirk. I can't stand it."

Her voice was rising in volume and becoming less controlled with each successive word she spoke. He walked towards her.

"I can't stand it," she repeated, softer this time. "I hate this fucking island. I hate these fucking crabs. I wish we could just fucking leave, I can't stand it here any longer."

He embraced her and she started sobbing openly. Leigh turned away to give the moment some privacy. He looked down at the crabs. It struck him as strange they would all gather along the shore like that. They had done it the night before, but that was when they were waiting for dusk so they could invade the land. But now it was still a long time before the sun would go down. Surely it was too early for them to gather along the shore.

His eyes followed the beach along the coast of the island. The thin line of white sand stretched far ahead, before finally giving way to rocks. A cliff steadily rose on the inner side to tower high over the beach. The strip of sand ended just under the ruins, right in front of the cave he had spotted from the boat. He wondered if the crabs lined the shoreline all the way across. If last night's numbers were any indication, it was very possible.

He squinted up at the ruins. He could not see much of the ruins from this distance or angle. He wondered what Andy and Inge were up to. He was probably forcing her to take pictures of him while he boasted about how many followers he had. Typical Andy.

Leigh turned his attention back to Dirk and Marianne. She seemed to be calming down, though her eyes continued to dart nervously between him and the lurking shadows in the water.

"Hey, you guys want to go and explore the cave with me?" Leigh asked.

Dirk raised an eyebrow to Marianne. He was leaving the decision to her. She sighed.

"Sure," she said at last, "it's not like we can go for a swim or anything."

Dirk motioned for Leigh to lead the way. Leigh turned and started walking along the beach. He, too, could not help glancing nervously at the malignant forms of the crabs in the clear waters. He was grateful they had buried their legs and claws in the sand, as seeing them would be just too creepy. He tried thinking of Inge to distract himself, but the accursed crabs would not leave his mind. He was sure they were waiting for something, but what it was he could not guess.

The cliff started to rise up on the side of the beach. They passed into the shadow of the cliff, and it was welcomely cooler than under the burning sun. Leigh glanced again at the waters. The crabs seemed to be clustered thicker here, and the space between their shells was at a premium.

Leigh continued to lead when doubts started nagging his mind. On one side of him, the water was thick with nasty, crawling crabs. On the other side, a rocky cliff face stretched up to the sky. He eyed the cliffs cautiously, suddenly feeling as though he was walking into a trap. There was no way he could scale that cliff. There were not enough handholds, and he was not an experienced climber. He glanced back at the crabs in the water, realising that if they wanted to come ashore, they would have all three of them trapped against the cliffs.

Stop it, he told himself, you cannot think like that. Think of them like Andy does. They are just crabs, and crabs are scavengers. They will not come out of the water and attack. He bit his lip, knowing he was unable to convince himself of the fact.

He turned to look back at Marianne and Dirk. Dirk had his arm around her and held her tight. She was trying to stare forward, but her eyes kept darting back to the crabs in the water. Leigh wondered if it had occurred to her how trapped they were just now.

As Leigh turned back, he spotted a crab on the sand just ahead of him. Leigh stopped. The crab had its back to him and had not spotted him yet. Its carapace was almost six inches in diameter and was coloured a sickly blue-grey.

"Is something wrong?" Dirk asked from behind.

Leigh half turned his head, ensuring he kept his eye on his quarry.

"All good, just a crab on the sand ahead. No problem, we can just skirt around him." Leigh tried to keep his voice steady, hoping his fear was not evident in his voice. He was glad Andy was not here, he would probably be making fun of him in this moment.

Leigh stepped forward and the crab scuttled about to face him. Leigh's stride broke, and the injury to his calf where the other crab had nipped him last night began to ache. He resisted the urge to rub the area, knowing the sudden aching was psychologically activated.

The crab raised itself to its full height and raised its claws aggressively as Leigh took another step forward. Leigh backed away slightly, his back making contact with the rocky cliff as he circled the aggressive crab. Now Andy would definitely be making fun of me, Leigh thought, now that the crab has me pressed up against the cliff.

Thankfully for Leigh, the crab made no move forward as he slid along the cliff face to pass it. He looked back to Dirk and Marianne, half expecting mockery in their eyes, but there was none.

"I don't like this," Marianne complained, "maybe we should just go back."

"But the cave is right there. Stand behind me if this guy worries you."

Dirk stepped in front and began circling the crab. It scuttled about to face him, again lifting itself to its full height in a show of aggression. Marianne put her hands on Dirk's shoulders and matched him step for step, like two dancers in a macabre shuffle, as he skirted the crab. The crab remained motionless, with only its eyestalks moving to follow them as they passed.

Dirk and Marianne passed the crab and moved up to beside Leigh. Dirk let out a large breath and Leigh realised that Dirk had been holding his breath the whole time they had been passing the crab. Dirk cast him a quick glance, realising now how obvious it was.

"I have to admit," Dirk said, "I did think this island was cool and different at first, but all these crabs are now starting to give me the heebie-jeebies as well."

"Welcome to the club," Leigh said dryly.

They backed away from the crab, which slowly lowered its claws and settled back into the sand. Leigh glanced into the water and spied the malevolent shapes of more crabs in the water. Here, however, he could see their legs clearly. Clouds of sand stained the water where they pulled free. It seemed like they were readying themselves to move.

Leigh glanced back along the beach to where they had come from. The cliff towered above him and stretched a long way along the beach. He suddenly felt like running. He looked nervously back at the crabs in the water, expecting at any moment for them to rush forward. But they remained silently in the water. Watching. Waiting.

Suddenly Leigh sensed space beside him and realised Dirk and Marianne had moved on. He turned to see them approach the cave. Dirk was a few steps ahead of Marianne and was approaching the cave entrance. Leigh shuffled forward quickly to catch up with them.

The cave was mostly shrouded in darkness. As Leigh approached, he could see a large grey boulder sat just outside the entrance. A second boulder, almost as big as the first, lay in front of the first. Dirk ran forward and jumped up onto the first boulder. He took a couple of steps then turned.

"Hey," he called, "there's a row boat in here. Maybe we could push it out and go fishing?"

Leigh suddenly felt a surge of hope. A boat did not just mean fishing, a boat could be a means of escape. They were no longer pinned to the island, trapped inside a prison surrounded by the ocean and the crabs. Leigh quickened his pace towards the cave, passing Marianne who had slowed and was looking up the cliff face.

"Hey, am I already hallucinating or are those really there?" Marianne asked.

Leigh stopped and turned to see Marianne pointing upwards. He followed the line of her finger to see she was pointing to a spot on the cliff directly above the boulder where Dirk stood. Sitting on a rock, slightly jutting out from the face eighteen feet above the beach, amid a jumble of sharp, jagged protuberances, Leigh could see exactly what had her so befuddled. It was a fresh bunch of bananas.

Dirk watched them curiously for a moment as they stared dumbfounded at the find before leaping down from the rock and trotting over to join them.

"Bananas," he pronounced as though he had just solved some great puzzle for them.

"Do you think they are ours?" Marianne asked.

"They must be. Where else could they have come from?"

"But how did they get up there?"

"The crabs put them there. Or something. I don't know. Does it really matter? It's food when we thought we had none. We can't just leave them there. We have to go up and get it."

Dirk walked over to the cliff face and felt around the rocky crevices for hand holds before leveraging himself up off the ground.

"You can't climb up there," Marianne gasped.

"I'm not leaving the only food on the island up there to rot."

"But it doesn't look safe."

"I'll be fine. This is just like climbing in the playground as a kid."

Dirk did not wait for Marianne's next words of protest and pushed himself up the rockface. She bit her lip, eyes darting from the bananas to Dirk and back again.

"Ok, but if it gets too hard, come back. I don't want you risking a broken neck over bananas."

Dirk said nothing in response and continued his climb. For the first six feet or so, Dirk had been correct. There were plenty of cracks in the face for hands or feet to fit into and the climbing was easy. But as he edged higher up, the cracks became fewer and far between.

Dirk was quite high above the beach when he found himself stuck without a next hand hold. He puzzled for a moment, staring up at the rocky wall above him. Then he spotted it; a small, smooth nook high to his right. He reached out, but the nook was a few inches out of reach. He would need to jump to reach it.

He searched around the wall more, searching for an alternative route, but none came to view. He looked up at the bananas. They were tantalisingly close now. If he grabbed hold of the nook, it would be just a short climb beyond that to reach them.

"If you're stuck, just come back. We can find another way to get them," Marianne called from below.

Dirk's stomach growled as he considered the nook. If he grabbed it, he would have nowhere to put his feet and would be momentarily hanging in space, but if he could get both hands in there he could quickly swing across and get his foot onto a sharp rock to the right. Once he got a foot on that sharp rock, he could step up and reach another crack. The bananas sat on a rock just above the crack. They were too close to give up on now.

Leigh and Marianne had been watching closely from below. Leigh had been studying the rockface and had calculated what Dirk was intending to do. As Dirk crouched slightly in preparation for the jump, he heard Marianne take a sharp breath in through her teeth. Clearly, she saw the risk too.

Dirk leapt.

His feet lost contact with the wall, and his only contact with the rockface was through his left hand. For a moment he seemed to hang in the air, Jordan like. His splayed fingers reached up, desperate for the touch of rock as he reached for the nook. And then he grabbed it.

Dirk's face and chest slammed into the rocky wall but he held on. He focused on getting a better grip of the nook, then let go of the cliff with his left hand to bring it up to the nook as well.

Marianne gasped, wishing to look away but also unable to do so. Dirk now hung precariously high above by his hands only.

Dirk twisted his body to look at his next target: the sharp rock jutting out to his right. He would have to start swinging like a pendulum from this spot to reach out to it. His hands and shoulders had begun to ache from the stresses of the climb, and he knew he could not afford to hang here long. He adjusted and tested his grip, ensuring his hands had a good hold, and then began to move his legs left to right to generate momentum.

Dirk's movements were as smooth as a gymnast's, and soon he was swinging nimbly from the nook. He reached out with his right foot, slightly brushing the sharp rock with the sole of his shoe. He just needed a little more momentum and he could do it.

Leigh frowned as he saw the sudden movement above Dirk. At first, he failed to make out what it was, as it was well camouflaged against the grey rock walls of the cliff. But as it scuttled sideways across the nook, there was no doubt in his mind that it was a crab. He could not see it well, but it looked to be dragging a claw at least six inches long. It closed on Dirk's hands, and as it raised its claws, Leigh felt a sudden dread wash over him.

Dirk felt something brush against his fingers. He was too focused on keeping his momentum going and the touch barely registered, but as he swung towards sharp rocks, pain scoured his hand as something hard and sharp closed tight around it. The pain weakened his grip, and his hands slipped from the nook. As he fell, he stretched out his foot towards the sharp rock. His foot missed. The momentum of the swing, however, carried him onto the rock. It hit him just above the knee, immediately cutting into his skin. He continued to fall, and a great rent was cut into his leg up to his groin before catching on the bone of his hip.

Dirk barely had time to register his leg had been opened when his body was violently thrown upside down with the momentum of his leap. His body spun like the point of a compass, its centre his skewered leg on the rock, and the back of his head to be slammed into the cliff. Marianne screamed as the senseless Dirk hung above her from his torn and bleeding leg. For a moment he just hung there, hovering high above while Marianne and Leigh watched in stunned silence below. A line of blood ran from behind his ear and across his forehead before finally dropping and spotting the sand below. Seconds later, his limp body fell and landed in a tumble of limbs a couple of feet from Leigh.

At the moment of impact with the ground, the shoreline burst alive with movement. The army of crabs that had lain in wait along the water's edge now rushed forward onto land in a flurry of spindly legs and bony shells. They raised their claws and clicked them, raising the ticking sound that was so familiar the night before.

Marianne screamed as the horde crawled forwards towards the inert body of Dirk. With horror, Leigh glanced up to see the crab in the nook clicking its claws victoriously.

Leigh jumped forward and grabbed Dirk by the wrist. He turned and began to drag the limp body behind him. Dirk's leg had been gouged and torn badly where the rock had caught him, and blood poured profusely from the ugly wound leaving a thick crimson trail painted across the sand behind him.

"Run," he screamed to Marianne. For a second she hesitated, her mind still foggy with the horror around her. "Fucking move it!"

The second shout seemed to have gotten through. She blinked, watching Leigh dragging Dirk through the sand, before turning and fleeing.

The horde of crabs turned in pursuit of their stolen meal. Leigh dared a glance over his shoulder and saw the crabs were converging on him in the hundreds. Maybe thousands. Even more were breaking from the shoreline as he watched.

Leigh started jogging. It was hard to move quickly with the deadweight of Dirk behind him dragging across the sand like an anchor, but the voracious swarm of clacking crabs provided the impetus he needed. He built up speed, his legs pumping hard with the strain.

Marianne screamed again and Leigh looked up. Crabs were breaking free of the banks ahead of them too, crawling out to block their path. Leigh edged away from the waterline and closer to the cliff, pushing himself to run even faster. But it was apparent the crabs would soon head them off, and within less than a minute they would no longer be running from them, but running through their vile ranks.

Leigh quickly glanced behind to see the streaming horde remained in pursuit.

"Whatever happens," Leigh yelled to Marianne between gulps of breath, "just keep running. If you stop, they'll drag you down through weight of numbers."

Ahead, Leigh could see the crabs had closed the gap between the cliff and water. Marianne's steps faltered as she realised there was no way forward.

"Run over them," Leigh shouted again.

He looked up. The cliff face still stretched above him, far too much for him to climb, especially encumbered as he was with the limp body of Dirk. He wondered for a moment if there was any point in continuing to drag Dirk along. Dirk may already be dead, and all he was achieving by dragging Dirk along like this was slowing himself down and risking his own chance of survival. But did he have it in him to just let go of Dirk and run? No, he could not do it. He could not face Inge and tell her he left her friend to the clutches of the ravenous crabs.

Marianne was now amongst them. She started prancing strangely as she tried picking out gaps of sand between crabs to place her feet. Claws snapped around her as she leapt from side to side. One claw closed on the sinew behind her knee and she shrieked madly. She staggered, almost falling down into them, but she thrust her leg out and placed her hand against the cliff to maintain balance. There was a crunch underfoot but she moved on before seeing what damage she had caused.

Leigh ran into the army of angry snapping claws. He did not bother looking where he placed his feet but ran heedlessly on. A couple of times he almost lost balance as he careened through the mob, but surprisingly few were snapping at him or trying to latch onto him with their claws as the other crab had done the day prior. As he pushed forward, though, he noticed his load growing gradually heavier behind him. He dared a glance behind, and realised Dirk's body had taken on a number of stowaways. Most of them clung grimly onto Dirk's clothes or a pinch of reddening skin to be dragged alongside, but some had clambered on top of the body and were hitching a ride in comfort. One crab, more ambitious and aggressive than the others, began clawing its way up Dirk's arm towards Leigh's hand.

Leigh turned and pumped his legs, dragging his burden on. Marianne sounded as though she was sobbing, and Leigh could see three crabs had now latched onto her hanging from their claws that dug deeply into the meaty parts of her legs.

The cliff was much lower here, and soon they would be able to leap up and run inland. As the cliff passed below the line of his head, he could see Andy and Inge running down towards them.

Suddenly there was sharp pain in his wrist. His grip on Dirk almost faltered, and he turned to see the crab that had been clambering up Dirk's arm now had its sharp pincers closed around the tendons of Leigh's wrist. The skin had been punctured and began to bleed.

Leigh gritted his teeth. He looked over to Inge, running down towards him in just a bikini top and shorts with her glorious body on display. He hoped she saw him, a hero, continuing to drag Dirk despite the raking pain he felt.

Andy reached the cliff edge just ahead of Marianne and held a hand out.

"Grab on," he shouted. She reached a hand up and latched onto his. She braced her foot against the rocks and he swung her up clear of the beach.

Pain seared Leigh's arm as the crab's second claw took hold of a pinch of flesh. He unwittingly let out a cry of pain. Leigh turned and cursed as the crab released one claw and reached further up his arm to clamp down on another piece of flesh. God, Leigh thought, it's climbing up my arm!

"Keep running to the end," Andy shouted.

Leigh had run past them now as they removed the crabs that clung to Marianne's legs. The cliff was waist high to Leigh now. He could jump up with help, but they were attending Marianne and he could not drop Dirk. Not with Inge now seeing him.

The crab on his arm closed its claw on the skin on the back of his elbow and edged further upwards. He glanced at it, and it raised its other claw towards his face, snapping it shut a mere couple of inches from his eyes. Leigh stepped on an uneven patch of ground, possibly a crab, and a pain laced his ankle. He ran on, pains now lacing his arm, wrist, ankle and legs while his calves burned with fatigue.

The cliff finally dropped away completely and Leigh took his first step off the sand onto the trim grassland of the island. Andy ran towards him, jumping with his arms outstretched and howling like a great ape.

"What are you doing?" Leigh heard Inge yell.

"Trying to scare the crabs," he replied before continuing the show. It would have been comical but for the grimness of the situation. "Look, it's working," he yelled a second time, "they are starting to fall back."

Leigh was relieved to hear it, but did not stop. The crab on Leigh's arm had reached his shoulder now and Leigh did not dare to turn, knowing his face would now be in range of those sharp claws. He felt a pain in his ear as the crab latched on.

That was it. He could not take it anymore. He let go of Dirk and tore at the crab on his ear. He pulled it off, and in his desperation tore the flesh of his ear away with the claw. Blood began to flow as he threw the crab to the ground and began stomping it, its hard shell crunching under his feet satisfyingly. There were more on his legs, and he turned to see there were at least ten riders still on Dirk's body when Andy drew up to it. Leigh looked back to the beach. The other crabs had ceased their pursuit for now.

Leigh attended to the crabs on his legs. One, in particular, was reluctant to be removed, twisting its claw and gripping harder to the fold of skin until Leigh crushed it between two stones from the ground. His legs were covered with thin red lines, some seeping blood, and small punctures where the crabs had latched on. His legs twinkled with a thousand pains from the cuts.

Andy pulled the last of the crabs free from Dirk's body and kicked it like a football back to the beach. Marianne approached gravely as Andy turned over Dirk's unmoving form.

Dirk's leg continued to bleed badly and his skin had taken a very pale shade. The continued bleeding, though, was a good sign that he was still alive, though maybe barely so. His skin had been scraped raw in many places across his arms, legs and stomach from the long drag across the sand. There were multiple cuts and lacerations from where the crabs had clutched at him with their claws, some crusted with sand but thankfully none as deep or bleeding as profusely as the deep laceration on his leg. His eyes were closed, and there was swelling around his eyes and blood in his mouth. One of his arms (not the one Leigh had dragged him by) also seemed to be bent unnaturally along the forearm and may also have been broken.

"Does anyone have bandages?" Andy yelled as he knelt down beside Dirk.

Leigh dropped to his knees, exhausted.

"Not enough for this," Marianne said between gasping breaths, her voice surprisingly steady. Shock had not set in yet.

"Then bring me some clothes. T-shirts, pants, whatever. Just bring me something to tie up this wound."

Leigh gasped at the air and felt weak. He was sweating profusely and it did not matter how much air he breathed in it did not feel like enough. His head swam and he began to rock from side to side, suddenly feeling nauseous. Suddenly, he toppled forward, blacking out completely.

16

Soft voices murmured around him. He struggled to make sense of the words. He recognised them individually, but strung together they jumbled and confused him. He tried to reach out and take hold, but it was like clutching a handful of water and the words fell away like drops between his fingers. He recognised one voice, but he could not place the source. Memory teased him, dancing out of reach tauntingly. Then it came to him. It was Andy.

There were other voices too. Strangely accented voices. Where were they? He tried to remember. Scent came to him. The sea. He started to remember. The trip. The sea. The foreign accents. He must be in the hostel in Bocas Town.

Leigh opened his eyes. The brightness seared at his retinas and he needed to blink as he adjusted to the light. Blue sky soared overhead, and Leigh became aware of the heat of the sun, the aches of his leg and ear, and the hunger of his stomach. And then the memory came back to him.

"Are you all right there, mate?"

Leigh pulled himself up and stared blankly about him. Andy and Inge were sitting on a backpack not far from him. They were sitting close, and their knees gently rested against one another. Leigh blinked at them and then looked about.

Dirk lay not far from him, and Marianne leaned over him to place a damp cloth on his head. Worry lines scoured her forehead as she tended her unresponsive patient.

"What happened?" Leigh groaned.

"You fainted after dragging Dirk up from the beach," Andy said.

"Yes, and luckily Andy was there to clear away the crabs and bring you and Dirk back to camp," Inge added.

Leigh grimaced. What the hell? He had dragged Dirk the whole length of the beach with thousands of crabs assailing him and somehow Andy is the hero? He swallowed. His throat felt dry and painful.

"Can I have some water?"

Andy picked up a bottle and tossed it his way. Leigh's mind was still clouded, and the bottle landed on his stomach. He grunted and gave Andy a foul look.

Leigh opened the bottle and gulped the water down greedily, easing the pain of his parched throat. After a few mouthfuls, he sat up properly and drank some more. When he finished, he turned to examine Dirk.

The cuts and scrapes that lined his body had been cleaned and had begun forming scabs. Some shone with freshly applied ointment. His skin was pale except where there was significant bruising. The bruises were ugly blue and yellow patches that contrasted malignantly against his pale skin. His arm had been tied to a length of firewood, though to Leigh's eye it still did not look perfectly straight. Finally, his leg was tightly wrapped in a makeshift bandage of torn t-shirts and jumpers.

"How's he doing?" Leigh croaked.

"He's weak," Marianne responded without looking up. A tear fell from one eye and landed on his chest. Leigh decided to look away, and turned to Andy. He did not like how closely Andy sat to Inge.

"We were just discussing," Andy said, ignoring what appeared to be a scowl forming on Leigh's face, "what we do about tonight."

Leigh raised an eyebrow. "And?"

"And," Inge cut in, "Andy thinks we should stay here while Marianne and I think we should move into the ruins. The ruins have higher walls and will be easier to defend if the crabs come back."

Leigh snorted. "There's no question of 'if'. They'll be coming back." Leigh rubbed his temples. His head ached. "Did Marianne tell you what happened down there?"

"Yeah, she told us. It sounded like a pretty risky climb as it was. But he was pretty unlucky that a crab was up there."

"Well, that's the thing. I don't think that crab was up there by accident."

"What do you mean?"

"Well," Leigh continued, slowing to get his thoughts collected and ordered, "those bananas up there, they had to be ours. They were taken from us last night. How do you think they got up there? And when Dirk climbed up the wall, there just happened to be a crab waiting at the point of the critical leap he had to make. And then all those crabs in the water, watching and waiting…" his voice drifted away.

"And?" Andy asked impatiently.

Broken from his reverie, Leigh looked up. "I don't know. It was strange being there. It was like… like they had it all planned. Like the crabs had put the bananas deliberately as bait and sat back and waited. Dirk just stumbled into a trap."

Inge gulped and looked away. Andy studied him closely, taking a long deep breath through his nose then letting it out slowly.

"OK," Andy said slowly, "I have a news flash for you here. Crabs aren't that smart."

"Well," Leigh grumbled, "you explain it then. You tell me how those bananas got there and why they were all lined up on the shore like that."

Andy opened his mouth and then closed it again. He looked around, and both Marianne and Inge were watching him anxiously. Andy shrugged. "I guess it could all be coincidence?"

Leigh snorted and shook his head.

"So, what are you saying, Leigh? The crabs are setting traps for us? For what purpose?"

"Well," Leigh started, licking his slips slowly, "last night they ate all our food. What if they are still hungry? What do they eat next?"

Andy stared at Leigh, blinking slowly. "Are you seriously suggesting the crabs are setting traps to kill and eat us? That's what you're saying, aren't you, Leigh?"

Leigh nodded.

"Jesus, Leigh, do you realise how crazy that sounds?"

Leigh stood up, suddenly flushed with anger. "What's so crazy about it? Last night, the crabs ate everything we have. They even cut through cans of beer. Now before seeing it for myself, I would have considered that crazy too. But that was real. It happened. And all those crabs out there, they are still hungry. Look around the island. There is nothing here. Absolutely nothing. You know why? Because the crabs already ate everything. Every animal, bird, insect and plant that was once here. Everything. That's why they came ashore in big numbers last night. They were ravenous. And now they've eaten all our food, what is left on this island when those hungry crabs come ashore at dusk tonight to feed? Us, mate. Only us. So now tell me again how crazy I sound when I say they mean to kill us."

As Leigh had talked, the volume and hysteria in his voice had increased to near panic levels. By the time his red-faced rant had finished, he was wide eyed and visibly shaking. Had they been anywhere but this island, he would have been immediately ushered into a strait jacket by men in white coats. But here, his rant seemingly made perfect sense.

Andy swore and placed his face in his hands. Inge reached forward, leaning into him as she did so, and pulled his hands away from his face.

"We have to go to the ruins," she said, "we're far too exposed out here with just our backpacks to make walls around us. We'd be like sitting ducks."

"I agree," said Marianne.

"But if we go up there, we close off two sides to cliffs. We'd essentially be cornering ourselves up there too."

"We'd be cornered out here. Don't you remember they had us completely surrounded last night?"

"But at least we'd be able to up and run away, even if it meant running through them."

"Run where?" Leigh cut in. "There is nowhere to run, or haven't you worked that out yet?" The words came out gruff. He was grumpy, and his voice harsher than he intended.

Andy stood and looked about him. He pursed his lips. "You don't think the ruins could just be another trap?"

Leigh gave him a dark look.

"Fine," Andy conceded. "I don't like it, but it appears I'm outvoted three to one. Let's shift our camp to the ruins."

Leigh hefted his bag up and turned to study the camp. "Hey Andy, maybe we should carry the bags up first while the girls look after Dirk."

"I can carry my own bag," Inge said.

"Uh, I just meant maybe you should keep Marianne company."

Inge gave him a doubting look but then shrugged. She stood up, letting Leigh pick up her bag and start walking up the hill. Andy picked up two bags and started following. He jogged a little to catch up to Leigh.

"If that 'we'll carry your bags' crap was meant to be chivalry, it was a pretty shit effort," Andy commented as he drew alongside.

"It wasn't chivalry. I wanted to speak with you alone," Leigh said without looking at his friend.

"Ok, what about?"

"Tell me what's going on."

Andy's eyes narrowed as he stared at Leigh. "What do you mean?"

"You and Inge all of a sudden seem much closer." Leigh turned to face Andy now. "Why is that?"

Andy let out a sigh. "Jesus, Leigh, not this crap again. Not now of all things."

"What crap?"

"This jealousy crap. Every time I get friendly with a girl you like you turn into some green headed jealousy monster. With all that is going on right now with this island, we don't need you bringing that crap to the table as well."

"You flirt with girls to make them like you over me," Leigh accused.

Andy rolled his eyes. "Flirting with girls doesn't make them like you."

"I know that, it's just… this better not be a repeat of what happened with Carly."

Carly. The very mention of her name was like tearing a scab from an old wound. Their friendship had almost completely ended over Carly. Mates since first grade, Andy and Leigh had exchanged blows over her. It was a fight that left Andy with cracked ribs and a swollen eye. Leigh was bigger and stronger, and Andy had to lump it.

Andy saw the situation as a love triangle. Leigh liked Carly. Carly liked Andy. Only in this triangle, Andy had slept with Carly, and Leigh caught them in bed together when he arrived to visit him the next day.

Leigh did not see it the same way as Andy though. All he saw was Andy had stolen Carly from him. Andy had learned all about Carly from Leigh. He knew exactly what to say to impress and seduce her. True, Leigh had yet to even kiss Carly, but on the night Andy had swept her away, Leigh was planning to open up to confess his feelings for her. That night should have gone very differently, and it should have been Andy catching Leigh and Carly in bed together the next day.

For a month they did not speak. Andy tried reaching out many times to heal the rift. He told Carly they could not go out. They liked each other a lot, and there was a lot of potential for a long-term relationship, but he turned her away for the sake of his friendship. One that slowly and steadily healed, but clearly still bore the scar of that first innocent, drunken tryst.

"Shit, Leigh, I don't know how many times I have to say it but I'm sorry about what happened with Carly. We really need to move on from that. Why would you go and bring her up again now? This has nothing to do with that situation."

"Ok, fine, this has nothing to do with Carly," Leigh pouted, "but everything to do with Inge. You have history in stealing from me and you seem awfully close with Inge all of a sudden. What did you do with Inge up in the ruins?"

"Nothing."

"Nothing?" Leigh raised an eyebrow.

"We took some photos for my social pages. That's all."

"You swear that was all that happened?"

"Yeah, I swear it," Andy answered.

They walked on in silence for a while. Leigh was barely conscious of his surroundings as they walked. He was too deep in his thoughts. They arrived at the ruins and dumped the bags.

It was the first time Leigh had seen the ruins and at first glance, it did seem like a fairly unsafe place to spend the night. As Andy had said, the building was set right against the cliff, and those walls that did line the cliff did not look very stable. The stonework in some places was not high, barely a foot more than the height of the bags they used the night before. They would have to set the fire in the open space where the doorway once sat, but aside from that, it was a little more defendable than the open space they used the night before.

"Not much to photograph," Leigh said dryly, turning away to walk back down the hill. Andy watched him a moment through narrowed eyes before slowly following him down.

17

It took just under an hour to move all their possessions and the injured Dirk up to the ruins. It took all four of them to carry Dirk to ensure he was properly supported. Leigh felt sick at the touch of Dirk's skin. It was hot and clammy, and Leigh had to cover his disgust. It felt like touching a dead man.

Andy ran an inventory of the firewood and estimated they had enough to see out the coming night. He tried to joke that maybe Leigh not taking his shift last night worked to their advantage in that way. The joke fell flat. Nobody wanted to be reminded of Leigh's error, particularly as it was the reason no one had eaten since dinner the day before and hunger clawed at their stomachs.

Andy then suggested trying to catch some crabs to cook and eat. Everyone agreed in principle, but as Andy laid out his plans to catch crabs (wading into the water on the beach and picking them up) their excitement cooled rapidly and he soon found no one would join him on the venture so he gave it away.

"I'd rather eat dirt than walk in the water with them," Marianne said. "Besides, we can't start a fire now, you said we might only just have enough to get through the night as is."

And so they all sat, huddled in the ruins, occasionally eyeing the surrounding area nervously for any adventurous scout crabs that may wander their way. The sun sapped their energy and their spirits were low. Conversation was minimal and the atmosphere was as grave as a funeral.

At one point, Inge sat close to Andy but, upon spying the suspicious stare cast in his direction from Leigh, Andy became restless and got up to pace the ruins a couple of times before sitting on his own in a different spot. Inge watched him pace, and frowned as he sat away from her. Leigh watched this all play out, glaring at them through it all.

Marianne stayed at Dirk's side, patting his brow with a damp cloth to keep him cool and occasionally pouring some water in his mouth and tickling his neck to engage the swallowing reflex. For the most part, Dirk lay as still as a corpse and as unresponsive as a rock. Marianne was running her fingers through his hair when he let out a slight groan. The sound was slight and small, but it drew everyone's attention immediately. He groaned again and started shaking his head slightly back and forth. His brow furrowed, and he groaned a third time.

"What's happening?" Leigh asked. "Are you doing something to him?"

Marianne pulled her hands away from him and gave him space. He groaned again, this time jerking his wounded leg at the same time.

"It's like he's in pain," Inge said.

"Hardly surprising, that leg was a mess and we have no anaesthetics."

"But still…" her voice trailed off as he groaned once more.

Suddenly his wounded leg jerked violently, kicking out hard against the stone wall of the ruins. He cried out, but his eyes remained shut. His whole body began to roll side to side as his wounded leg jerked and kicked repeatedly.

"Something's wrong," Marianne stated. "Do you think you wrapped the wound right?"

Andy scratched his head. His eyes started to betray worry as he bit his lip. "I think so. I mean, I did the best I could with what I had."

"Maybe it's too tight?" Inge suggested.

"No, it needed to be tight to stem the bleeding."

Dirk began to rock more violently, his foot kicking divots of dirt up from the ground.

"Then what?"

"I don't know," Andy replied, his face turning red as he became visibly flustered.

Marianne continued patting Dirk's head with a cloth and in a low voice uttering calming words, but it was not use. Dirk's cries became louder and the shaking of his wounded leg became more vigorous and violent.

"We have to do something," Marianne pleaded.

"OK," Andy said, coming to a conclusion, "I think we should undo the bandages and check his wound."

"Then do it."

"Ok, I'll need you guys to try to hold him still for me."

Leigh and Inge approached Dirk and crouched beside him. Leigh held onto Dirk's wounded leg while Inge held the other. He tried smiling at her, glad to again be in close proximity with her once more, but her brief half smile response left him disappointed.

Andy began picking at the knot of clothing that held the makeshift bandages together. Dirk's leg again shuddered and Leigh adjusted his position to double-down his weight on Dirk to ensure no further movement. Andy eventually undid the knot and pulled the layers of clothing aside to reveal the sticky red mess that was Dirk's leg.

The wound stretched from just below the crotch to just above his knee. The flesh had been brutally gouged out, and the opening was at least two inches wide and at least double that deep. Leigh concluded the rock must have caught his leg near the knee, and as Dirk continued to fall with the momentum of his leap and gravity, the flesh of his leg tore open like a ripped envelope to the hip. Leigh wondered if there had been too much meat scooped away for it to grow back again properly.

"These will need to be replaced," Andy said, throwing the stained clothing aside. "The wound has been seeping the whole time. At least the flow of blood has stopped."

Leigh studied Dirk's pained face. It was very pale. He probably did not have much more blood left to lose.

"Pass me the water, we need to start cleaning."

Using a wetted t-shirt, Andy starting patting at the outside of the wound and cleaning the sticky red muck away. Dirk stayed mercifully still during the process.

"There," Andy announced at last, "all done. We just need to put some fresh bandages on and he'll be right."

Marianne rose and stepped across to her backpack and starting taking out t-shirts and dresses to use.

"But all you did was clean it. What could have made him kick and shudder like that?"

"I'm not sure. Maybe I didn't put the bandage on right or the knot was digging into his leg or something. I'll try and do it differently this time around."

Everyone seemed satisfied with Andy's response and relaxed. Andy started tearing strips of clothing while Leigh and Inge eased back from holding Dirk down when Dirk cried out once more, kicking violently with his injured leg and almost catching Leigh on the chin with his foot.

"Shit," Leigh swore.

"He's still in a lot of pain," Inge said

Andy scratched his head. "The pain should be constant, not coming in random peaks like that." He passed the torn strips back to Marianne. "I'm going to have to check inside the wound." Andy picked up a bottle. His face seemed to pale as he turned to Leigh. "Hold him tight, mate, he's going to kick hard at this."

Leigh put his weight on Dirk's leg and nodded. Andy poured water in the wound, filling it. Reddened water filled with congealed blood spilled from the wound. Dirk twitched. They shifted his body to empty the water out and Andy pulled the wound open to look inside. The pressure was making the wound fill with blood once more as he spied something small, grey and round in the wound that glistened with wetness.

He leaned back, breathing out slowly and swallowing hard.

"What's wrong?" Marianne asked.

Andy's eyes swivelled to meet hers as he sucked in a breath through his teeth. "I think," he said, speaking the words in a slow, calculated fashion, "that there is a crab in his leg. Small, maybe a baby. It's no bigger than my thumb, but a crab nonetheless."

Marianne paled, and turned to look at the wound with horror.

Dirk's leg shuddered once more. Leigh swallowed the lump that had been forming in his throat. These shudders from Dirk weren't from pain, but from what? That little crab moving about in there? Or worse, what if the crab was eating Dirk from the inside? Leigh began to feel ill, but whether it came from the hunger or the thought of that little crab eating the meat of Dirk's leg from inside the wound he could not say.

"We have to get it out," Marianne said.

Andy nodded. His eyes were fixed on the wound and his skin, too, seemed to be going grey.

"Does anyone have tweezers in their bags?" Andy asked.

He looked at each of them individually. They all shook their heads. Andy frowned. He stood and walked over to the ramshackle pile of possessions that had been dropped in the centre of the ruin. He sorted through the mess until he found some cutlery. He came back with two forks, a butter knife and a spoon. Inge muttered something in Dutch and turned away.

"I know how bad this looks, but it's the best I can do right now. I'm going to need you all to hold him tight. If he starts kicking, I'm only going to hurt him even more."

Leigh adjusted himself so that he sat on Dirk's shin and put his hands on Dirk's knee. His whole weight should hold this leg in place, he thought. Inge put her weight onto his other leg while Marianne held him around the shoulders.

Andy hesitated, checking with each one individually that they were ready before turning back to the wound. Andy looks like he is about to vomit, Leigh thought. Leigh licked his dry lips. He could hardly fault him if he did. He was just glad it was Andy going into the wound and not him.

Andy's shaking hand slid the butter knife down between the walls of gouged flesh. Dirk twitched.

"Try not to touch the sides," Inge suggested.

"I can't help it," Andy said, "and I think I will need to anyway to dig the bugger out."

Andy sloshed some water into the wound to clear the seeping blood away. He spotted the grey, pebble-like shape and pushed the knife towards it. The crab had wedged itself tightly into the meat of Dirk's leg, and Andy would have to push into the flesh to get the knife over it.

"Hold him tight, this will probably hurt," Andy said.

He pushed the knife between the wall of flesh and crab. A cry broke from Dirk's lips and he tried to sit up. Andy turned to help Marianne hold him and the knife fell away into the dirt.

"Shit," Andy swore. Dirk settled and Andy ran his hand through his hair.

"OK, change of plan. Leigh, you'll need to hold both legs and Inge, you come this end and support Marianne."

While everyone switched positions, Andy cleaned off the knife and took a sip of water. Leigh noticed Andy was sweating profusely, the wide wet patch of sweat under his arms was spreading rapidly through his t-shirt. Andy's face was also ashen and his lips dry, despite having just drunk.

"Here we go. Take two," Andy said as he opened the wound to push the butter knife in once more. He tipped water into the wound again to clear away the blood. Leigh watched the bloody water spill out, richer in colour than it had been previously. The bleeding had renewed intensity after the first aborted attempt. They needed to get the crab out quickly to prevent Dirk losing too much more blood.

"Ready?" Andy warned as he readied the butter knife. He waited a second before pushing the knife into the soft flesh above the crab. Dirk shuddered and tried to sit but the girls managed to hold him down. The muscle and tissue gave way, allowing Andy to wedge the knife between the crab and the meat of Dirk's leg. Next, Andy reached for a fork.

"What are you doing with that?" Leigh asked.

"I've got to grab the little bugger from both sides, otherwise I'm just pushing it into his leg."

Andy started sliding the fork down the opposite side of the wound. He held the knife steady with one hand and the fork with the other. His facial expression was a mask of concentration, and Leigh watched him oddly. It was like watching a child trying to use a knife and fork for the first time.

Dirk shuddered and Leigh pushed down on his leg harder.

"Shit," Andy swore, "the little bugger moved as soon as the fork touched its legs."

Andy sloshed more water through the wound. It splashed out, the water again cloudy and thick with blood. Andy took up the knife and fork once more and pushed into the soft meat of Dirk's leg. Leigh looked away. It was torturous just to watch.

Andy pushed his implements deeper into the wound, trying to get them on either side of the crab. This time he started by sliding the fork under the crab's legs. This time it did not move, and he started to slide the knife in over its head. He pushed the knife until it met hard resistance. The fork, he hoped, and not bone. He leveraged the two implements, aiming to hold the little crab between them and pull it out.

Sweat prickled his brow and a drop started rolling down his nose. It tickled, and he ached to brush it away. But he forced himself to focus and maintain his grip. He began withdrawing the knife and fork slowly, the little crab wedged in their grip. He let himself smile grimly. It was working. He was getting the crab out.

Then the crab turned around to face him. Andy barely had time to register it was not held tight between the two implements when the crab scuttled out of his grip and between two folds of flash in another part of the wound.

"Argh," Andy growled through gritted teeth, "I thought I had it there."

The stress was evident on Andy's face as he pushed the knife and fork into the wound once more. He was grimacing and his eyes were wide. The knuckles on his hands were white.

A second time Andy got the knife and fork around the crab's shell, but again it scuttled clear and pushed its hard carapace deeper between bleeding folds of soft muscle and tissue. Andy tried to follow it and grab it as it moved, but his fork caught in the torn meat of Dirk's leg. Dirk shuddered and Leigh and the girls had to push hard to hold him in place.

"Easy, mate," Leigh urged, "you'll do more damage than good that way."

Andy cursed. He wanted to stab the little bugger with his fork and pull it out that way. But it was too risky; he might stab an artery or create a deeper wound in the process. Andy closed his eyes a moment and took a deep breath to calm and fortify himself. He let the breath out slowly and opened his eyes once more.

Blood had welled up on the wound and he needed to rinse it out again. He poured in the water and watched it slosh out. Dirk's bleeding was becoming more pronounced.

"We can't leave that wound open like that much longer, he's bleeding too much," Leigh said.

Andy gritted his teeth. "I'm aware, mate. That commentary isn't helping."

The crab had crawled close to the knee now and Andy shifted his position to get closer. He pushed the fork into the opening but as the metal touched the crab, it skittered away once more.

Andy sat straight and breathed deep, gulping breaths.

"Leigh's right. This is taking too long. We need to find another way to get it out," Marianne said, her eyes brimming with tears.

Andy removed the blood-stained cutlery from the wound and turned to her. “OK, but how?”

“Use your fingers,” Inge suggested.

Andy looked at her and then back at the wound. He closed his eyes and swallowed. For a moment Leigh though he was about to say no, but Andy re-opened his eyes and set the knife and fork aside. He splashed water over his hands and into the wound once more. He put his hand next to the gaping wound, resting it there a moment before moving it in.

Dirk shuddered and Andy’s face grimaced as he started feeling his way into the wet tissue of the leg. It felt spongy and horrible, and Andy started dry retching as he pushed his fingers deeper into the crevasse of Dirk’s leg. He could not see in and felt his way into the wound. The meat enclosed his fingers, and he was forced to push down to get his fingers deeper in. Dirk shuddered and kicked.

“For God’s sake, hold him still,” Andy burst out. He clenched his eyes shut and pushed deeper into the flesh, trying to ignore the fact he may have been opening the wound more to fit his fat fingers in.

Finally, he struck something hard. He ran his fingers around it. It was small and round. He pushed his thumb deeper inside the wound, ignoring the spasmodic movements of Dirk’s leg as he did so. He had it trapped now, between his thumb and forefinger on one side, and the walls of flesh on the other.

He brought his thumb and forefinger together. He felt its little legs writhe as it tried to escape and he squeezed hard on its bony little body. It retaliated with its tiny claws, clamping onto the thin strip of skin at the top of his fingernail and tearing. Andy cried out in pain.

“Have you got it?” Marianne asked.

“Yes,” Andy answered through gritted teeth. The little bugger’s claws worked at Andy’s fingernail as he slowly withdrew his hand from the wound. Andy ignored the sharp pain and tried to focus on getting the crab out. At last, he pulled his hand clear and stood up. He marched to the cliffside edge of the ruins to throw the crab out to sea. He flung his arm, letting go of the small crab but it hung on.

He looked at his hand. The small crab’s oval eyes gleamed back at him. It had dug its claws under the skin at the back of the fingernail and was holding tight. Andy flicked his hand, trying to shake the little monster free but it held tight. Finally, he laid his hand on a rock and picked up a second rock to slowly bring it down onto the crab and crush it. The crab must have been aware of the danger, and at first touch of the rock it skuttled away.

The little crab was remarkably quick, crawling spider-like up one side of the ruin's wall and over the other. Andy stood up, leaning over the edge to watch it crawl out of view.

He turned to see Marianne and Inge had already moved to start the bandaging process of the leg. He heaved a sigh of relief. His heart was pumping hard and he slumped down to sit. He suddenly felt gravely ill, and he turned to one side to vomit. But his stomach was empty, and all he could bring up was rotten tasting bile that burned the back of his throat and could not be washed away.

18

After the crab was removed from his leg, Dirk's movements settled before stopping altogether at the completion of the re-wrapping of his leg. In fact, he lay as still as a corpse. Marianne cradled his head in her lap, constantly patting his head with a cloth, pouring small amounts of water into his mouth and checking the strength of his pulse. There was no hiding the distress in her face or the worry in her eyes.

"Are you sure there is no way we can call Jorge?" she asked for what seemed like the hundredth time. Nobody chose to answer her. They were wary of telling her no, and hated to constantly be the bearer of bad news.

Dirk had grown much paler since the crab extraction, his complexion now not far from being as white as paper. Leigh doubted Dirk would make it through the night. He had lost too much blood, both at the time of the incident and again with the crab extraction. Even as Leigh stared now, he could swear the blood stain on Dirk's bandages was growing.

Leigh started growing restless. The hunger-ache of his stomach was growing with every passing moment. The others were affected by it too. He heard the rumbling of Marianne's stomach, and she cast him a glance shortly after. Was she still blaming him over the incident last night? How could she? It was Andy who failed to wake him and it was Andy who brought them to the island to begin with. She should start finding faults in him for a change.

But it was not just the hunger that was getting to him. It was the boredom of doing nothing but sitting under the burning sun in a cluster of broken old bricks. Then there was the fear of what lay just below the water's surface all around the island, half buried in the sand. It was also knowing that they lay there waiting for dusk, and the knowledge of the inward march the army of crabs would happen again, when they would come looking for food and find only them. It was all becoming too much.

Leigh stood up and started pacing. He felt like a man on death row, knowing his execution was coming this night. But a man on death row got one final meal. Even a man on death row had it better than they did right now.

He cast a glance at Inge. He pondered her a minute. She gnawed a fingernail vigorously as her eyes darted about. Her skin shone with sweat and her worried eyes bore dark rings under them. She looked like she had aged ten years since arriving, but he still found her beautiful. He wondered if she too was considering that tonight may be her last night. Perhaps she might be interested in one last fling before she died. He had heard girls might be up for that. It would be as Andy had said, 'setting doesn't matter'. Maybe he could still have one over the death row inmate after all.

"Hey, Inge," he said, "do you fancy going for a walk with me?"

Her eyes glanced quickly to Andy, then up to Leigh. "No, I think I'd rather just stay here for now."

Leigh smiled thinly, then continued to pace. The death row inmate was still ahead on points.

That was another thing that was getting to him. Inge and Andy. He had watched them closely all day. Inge constantly looking Andy's way, moving close to him, only for Andy to pull away and look uncomfortable. Inge liked Andy. He hated to admit it, but the more he watched, the more he became convinced of it. Fucking Andy. He always treated girls as though their only purpose for was to put his dick in to get his jollies with and nothing more. He never treated them well, yet they all seemed to be drawn to him over Leigh. Why? Leigh was a nicer guy than Andy. He would treat a girl better if they gave him the chance. For Leigh, they were more than just some hole to fuck.

What could Andy give Inge that was better than what Leigh could? Andy would probably fuck her and say bye and she would never hear from him again. Leigh would not be like that. He would get her email address. He would write to her regularly. He would save up and visit her in Holland. Maybe he could even live with her there for a while. Who knows where that could lead, maybe even marriage? Leigh frowned. How could a one-night stand be better than that? Wasn't a nice husband what all girls wanted? Leigh could be that guy if only she gave him the chance.

Fucking Andy.

At least Andy was being good about it this time. He moved away whenever Inge moved close. Leigh had never truly gotten over the Carly incident. He still got angry about it now when he recalled what Andy did. So what if he had not even kissed her? He had loved her and Andy knew that. Him screwing her was the ultimate act of betrayal. At least he exposed her for the slut she was. That was probably the only good thing that came out of the whole affair. Sluts like that could not be trusted. Leigh kicked a rock angrily.

Inge frowned as she watched the rock clatter into the ruins wall not far from her. "Didn't you say you were going for a walk?" she asked.

"What?" he answered sharply.

"I thought you said you were going for a walk."

"No, I thought you might want to. That's why I offered."

"Oh."

Leigh watched her a moment. His stomach started feeling ill and he took another swig from the bottle of water he had been using. He wiped the sweat from his brow and looked at Inge again. He wished he could get her alone. To be able to talk to her. Tell her of his feelings. Make her see that he was the right guy for her, not Andy. Set her straight.

Leigh walked over to the edge of the cliff and looked over. It was a great view from this point. They were high, and the glittering sea stretched all the way to the horizon. But for Leigh, it was not a thing of beauty, but instead a reminder of how isolated they were. How far was the nearest human to us, Leigh wondered. It must be miles and miles. They may as well have been up in space for all it mattered. There was no way to communicate with anyone anywhere. For a moment he remembered Jorge and how quickly he left. Now he knew why, he could not blame him. He only hoped Jorge was true to his word and would come back.

Leigh looked down the cliff. It was a long distance down to the beach and cave below. He estimated the drop would be close to three hundred feet in total. There were a number of ledges sticking out from the cliff face. Many were covered in macabre, jagged shapes. There was also a lot of cracks and niches in the cliff face, much like the spot where Dirk had climbed and fallen. He supposed a professional rock climber could scale the cliff. Hell, they would probably even welcome the challenge. But not Leigh. To him those people were madmen.

Leigh was about to turn away when something colourful fluttering in the wind caught his eye. At first, he could not see it all that well. He walked along the edge of the cliff line to open up his view of it. The glare from the sun reflecting off the ocean momentarily gave him sunspots on his eyes, and he had to wait a moment for his eyes to adjust. But then as he stared at it, it became clear. It was a striped yellow and red t-shirt caught on one of the sharp rocks of the cliff.

He stopped a moment. It looked familiar, but he could not remember when he had seen it before or who had been wearing it. Then it came to him. Inge had been wearing it this morning. He remembered it well. It was loose around the neck, allowing him to glance down her top and see her cleavage every time she bent down to pick up a piece of rubbish during the clean-up. She had worn it as she had chased Andy up the hill too.

And then he remembered Andy and Inge racing towards him as he dragged Dirk off the beach. She only had her bikini top on then. No t-shirt.

He swivelled around to face them. Inge had moved over to Andy again, and they now stood close to each other and were speaking in low whispers. Andy saw Leigh turn and glanced nervously at him. Suddenly it all became clear to Leigh. Andy had betrayed him again.

Leigh's heartrate began to quicken. He was certain of it now. Andy, that God damn selfish son of a bitch, had taken Inge away from him. Just like he had with Carly. Fucking Andy. All he ever thought about was himself. It made sense that he was dedicating his life to being an influencer. It was the only profession in the world that enabled such self-adulating behaviour. What other profession was there that let you constantly post pictures, video and text about yourself and have others comment and admire you? It was no wonder Andy had such a warped sense of the world and thought everything was there for him to take and post about, including the girls that were meant for Leigh.

But how should he confront them?

Leigh thrust his hands in his pockets. He felt something hard with his left hand. He curled his fingers around the object, feeling its shape. It was a keyring. The clog keyring that Inge had given him the morning of the trip to Nivida. Had she not given him that keyring because she had liked Leigh back? Yes, she had. She had liked Leigh, they were getting along well, and then Andy had to come in and ruin it.

Fucking Andy.

"Are you alright, Leigh?" Andy asked.

Leigh blinked. He realised he had been staring at Andy and as he looked around now, everyone was staring at him.

"What?"

"I asked if you were alright. You were breathing heavy and sounded like you were about to have a stroke or something."

Leigh realised suddenly that he was breathing hard. Unconsciously he had been working himself up for a confrontation. He pulled his hands from his pockets and looked down to see his hands were shaking. He clenched them into fists. He and Andy had fought before. That was when Andy stole Carly from him. Leigh had bested Andy that day, he could do it again. He just needed Andy to admit the betrayal first. Then he would set Andy straight.

"I'm surprised you don't recognise the sound," Leigh sneered. "It's the sound someone makes when they've been stabbed in the back."

Andy glanced quickly at Inge and swore softly under his breath.

"That's right, Andy, I've worked it out. You're jealous of me, aren't you?" Leigh's voice began rising in volume and pitch as he spoke. "You see me fall in love, a feeling you are incapable of, so you ruin it for me. Every time. You just can't let me be with the girls I love, can you? No, you have to come in, fuck them first and spoil them for me."

Andy held up his hands placatingly. "Look, Leigh I think you need to settle down a bit, mate."

"Settle down?" Leigh roared, the words having the opposite effect than intended. "I don't need to settle down. You need to tell me the truth. You fucked her, didn't you?"

Andy and Inge exchanged a glance. Then Inge spoke up.

"Leigh, you need to know…"

"Shut up, slut," Leigh interrupted. "I don't want to hear from you. I want him to admit it. Andy, you cheated me again, didn't you?"

"It's not like that, Leigh, I never set out to…"

"Just admit you fucked her," Leigh yelled.

Andy gulped, his Adam's apple bobbing like a cork in the ocean. He glanced quickly to Inge then back to his friend. "Ok, yes, we had sex. It wasn't planned, it just happened."

Tears welled in Leigh's eyes while fury raged through his body. His mind was cluttered as hundreds of thoughts invaded his conscious. They all had the common thread: Carly, Inge, Andy and betrayal. He tried to speak, but he shouted a nonsensical sound instead. Frustrated, he picked up a rock and threw it.

The rock narrowly missed Andy.

"Hey," Andy cried, ducking after the rock had passed, "you need to settle down."

"No. You need to stop taking what is mine."

Inge went to speak but Andy held up his hand to stop her. Andy took a deep breath and studied his friend. Leigh was overheating, he needed to bring him down.

"Leigh, mate, no one intended to hurt you here. I know you like Inge. But liking a girl isn't the same as reserving a table at a restaurant. She needs to feel the same way as you."

"And she would, if you hadn't turned her against me."

"Nobody turned anybody against you, Leigh."

"Yes, you did. You planned it all along. From the moment you saw the wet clothes clinging to her body in Nivida, you were planning to steal her. And last night you took your chance. You pretended to wake me up so that when everyone woke in the morning, they would blame me for not protecting the camp."

Andy took a deep breath and turned away. He was starting to lose patience himself. He had been on the end of these wild accusations before. "I woke you, Leigh. We spoke. Nobody set you up. You just didn't get up."

"Stop it. Stop lying."

"I'm not lying."

Words failed him so Leigh roared like a crazed ape. He needed to release the anger building inside. He stooped down and picked up another stone and threw it wildly. It was a bad throw, hitting the ground and bouncing up to nick Inge's leg. She cried out in Dutch. A sliver of blood appeared almost immediately.

Andy took a step forward to stand between Leigh and Inge. He held out one hand in a stop sign.

"Leigh, mate, you need to calm down. Maybe you should go on that walk you wanted and cool your head."

"I only wanted to walk to get Inge alone. Now there's no point. Now I know she's a slut."

"Hey," Marianne yelled, "stop calling her that, you psycho."

Leigh bobbed down to pick up another stone and flung it at Marianne. It bounded a couple of feet in front of her, kicking up dirt as it bounced harmlessly past her. She looked up at him fearfully.

"Stop throwing stones. You're going to hurt someone."

"Make me."

Andy gritted his teeth and shook his head. "I don't want to fight you, Leigh. You're my best friend."

"You sure don't act like it. First Carly, now Inge. Some best friend you are."

Andy looked at him sadly. "You really don't get it, do you? I liked Carly. I mean, I really liked Carly. We spent all night in bed together that night before you caught us. We just lay there and talked and talked and talked. You think I'm some self-centred man-whore that likes to just fuck girls and leave them, but I'm not. I'm just looking for another connection like I had with Carly. She was… something else. And I gave her up for you. I gave her up because of how important my friendship is with you."

Leigh found his vision completely blurred with tears now, but the anger still burned inside like the fires of hell. He could not stand it anymore.

"No more lies," Leigh cried. He stooped down to retrieve and throw another rock. It smacked noisily against the stone wall of the ruin. He bent down again, but his eyes were too filled with tears for him to see clearly. He felt around for another rock to throw. Suddenly he heard footsteps running towards him. He stood in time to fend off Andy's initial grapple.

"Stop it," Andy yelled, "stop before you hurt someone."

Leigh pushed Andy back before throwing the first punch. It was a clumsy jab, thudding uselessly into Andy's shoulder. Andy tried grappling again, clutching handfuls of Leigh's t-shirt as he tried wrestling him to the ground. It was a stupid move; Leigh was not only bigger and stronger, but he was also like a raging bull and would not come down until it was finished. Leigh grabbed Andy with one hand while attempting to punch Andy in the stomach with the other. There was a sound of tearing fabric and Leigh pushed forward into Andy. Suddenly, he was toppling forward to land on his once best friend.

They landed with a grunt. Andy was winded, and his grip loosened enough for Leigh to roll away and get back to his feet with his fists at the ready. Andy groaned and rolled over to pull himself up. He put out a hand in a placating gesture.

"We need to stop this now," Andy said.

"No, you started this so now we have to finish it."

"You need to calm down."

"No, Andy. This time we finish the fight. The loser stays out here all night. The winner shares a sleeping bag with Inge."

"No, we're not doing that."

Leigh stepped forward to shove Andy in the chest. "Come on. What are you afraid of?"

"Inge is a person who makes her own decisions, not some prize you get to treat like that."

Leigh shoved Andy in the chest again, this time with more force. Andy stepped back. The back of his legs touched against something. It must have been the wall of the ruin.

Leigh stepped forward with a face masked in malice. He heard one of the girls shout something from behind him, but he was so focused on Andy he could not comprehend what she said. Andy paled. Good, he should be afraid. Leigh would finish this today, exacting out the punishment he owed Andy for stealing both Carly and Inge away from him.

Leigh stepped forward and swung a right hook. Andy raised his left arm to block, but the impact threw Andy off balance. Andy stepped back to maintain his footing as Leigh swung with his left. Suddenly there was nothing but empty air in front of Leigh. There was a female scream from behind. For a moment Leigh was disoriented. And then he realised what had happened. He had forced Andy over the edge of the cliff.

19

"Watch out, you're on the edge," Marianne called.

It had been for nought. Leigh swung and Andy, taken by the blow, tripped over the wall and fell backwards and out of sight.

Inge screamed, but neither her of Marianne dared to move. They shared a quick glance, and Marianne could tell Inge was just as frightened as she was. In less than half a day, their day had gone from a bad experience into a living nightmare. There was no food. There were thousands of creepy crawly crabs. Dirk may be dying. And now this.

Leigh had done it on purpose. Of that there was little doubt. She had given ample warning. Andy had heard her and acknowledged, but Leigh did not stop. He had tried to kill Andy, and may well have succeeded.

Marianne barely dared to breathe. She wished she could slink into the shadows and not be seen. She stared, waiting to see what Leigh would do next. But he did nothing for a long, long time. He just stood there, staring out into space.

Finally, after what seemed like an eternity, he turned. His face was red and his eyes blazed. He glared at Inge and then Marianne, but his face bore no recognition. He marched across the ruin, first to his bag to pull out his phone and a set of headphones, then spun purposefully around to march out of the ruins, down the hill and away from them.

Both Inge and Marianne wordlessly watched him leave. When he was a reasonable distance away, Inge ran to the cliff edge and looked over. Marianne dared not move from Dirk's side, afraid both of leaving Dirk's side and of what horror she would see if she looked over the edge.

Marianne placed her head in her hands. "God, what a fucking psycho." Her heart was hammering like a drum and her breathing was rapid. She sucked in a few deep breaths to try and calm her frayed nerves before looking up to see Inge crouched on the cliff edge. "Can you see him?" Marianne asked.

Inge looked down for a long time before pulling away from the edge and slumping down to sit. "This is all so surreal," she said, her voice giving the semblance of a trance-like state. "It's like a really bad dream."

"Did you see him?" Marianne repeated.

Inge looked up and for a moment seemed surprised to see Marianne sitting there. She blinked, nodded and then waved her hand vaguely towards the cliff. "He… he landed on a ledge about forty feet down."

"But… is he alive?"

"I think so. I mean… he's probably unconscious. It looked like he was breathing."

"Do you think we could climb down to him?"

Inge bit her lip. "No chance. It's far too risky. Plus, there's barely any room to stand on the ledge he's on."

Marianne swallowed the lump in her throat and turned to fuss over Dirk. There was no reason to attend Dirk, she just needed to turn away from Inge to hide the tears in her eyes. One tear dropped onto Dirk's cheek and she wiped it gently away from her thumb. Her nose threatened to drip too, and she wiped it with the back of her wrist. She put two fingers on Dirk's neck. His pulse was weak. She turned back to Inge.

"What are we going to do?" Marianne asked.

Inge looked about the clearing. "I think we make a rope by tying our clothes together. When he wakes up, we could lower it down and we could try pulling him up?"

Marianne shook her head. "I didn't mean that. I meant what are we going to do about that psycho Leigh? What are we going to do when he comes back?"

Inge looked blankly at Marianne a moment before a look of recognition passed across her face. She began chewing a nail, as she often did when she was nervous or in deep thought.

She's starting to get it, thought Marianne. She's finally realising that it was just the two of them and Leigh right now. And Leigh was not normal. They could not afford to feel safe around him any longer. Eventually Leigh would be back, whether by his own accord or driven here when the crabs came ashore at dusk, and it would be the two of them trapped with a madman. Marianne's skin crawled at the prospect.

Tears began to well in Inge's eyes now as she spat a piece of nail from her mouth. She stopped and looked at her friend. She forced herself to her feet and stumbled across the ruins to slump down beside Marianne. Inge looked at Marianne a second and then placed her arms around her.

"I'm sorry," she blubbered to Marianne.

"What for? This isn't your fault."

"No, it is my fault. I forced you to come here. And now Dirk's life is in danger because of it."

Marianne shook her head. "It's not your fault. Dirk wanted to come here too. He wanted something he could brag to his mates about. You getting the chance to hook up was an added benefit. We didn't come just for you."

"I know… God. Leigh seemed like such a decent guy at the start. How'd he go from nice guy to clingy jealous psychopath so quickly?"

"You sure do attract some strange ones."

Marianne wrapped her arms around Inge. It felt good to hold her. She clung to her tightly. It gave her warmth and strength.

"You know what the worst part of this is?" Marianne asked.

Inge shook her head.

"The worst part," Marianne continued, "is that you had sex with Andy and you didn't tell me about it."

Inge scoffed and wiped her eyes. "I think Leigh just killed any joy I could get out of retelling that story."

Inge untangled herself from Marianne and stood up. She glanced down the hill, then walked over to peer over the edge once more at Andy. She tapped her foot and lifted her hand to chew a nail. She then turned back to Marianne and crossed her arms.

"We can't go on like this."

"What do you mean?"

"I mean we can't just sit here and wait the day out. Leigh will come back. I can't spend the night trapped in this small space with him. Any of those rocks could have hit us before and he didn't care. If he's violent like that, there's no telling what he could try to do tonight when the pressure is on. No, I can't spend a night trapped here with him. I wouldn't feel safe."

"But what can we do?"

Inge pursed her lips and looked away. "We deal with him."

"Deal with him?"

"Yeah. You know…" Inge ran her finger across her neck in a throat-slitting gesture.

Marianne felt her blood run cold. "You can't be serious."

"I'm not. Or I am. I'm not sure. But if not that, what choice do we have? I can only think of two ways out of this. It's deal with him or escape the island and get away from him. And there's no getting off the island without a boat…"

"Wait," Marianne cried. She looked at Dirk and gulped, before turning back to Inge. "There is a boat."

"What? Where?"

"In the cave at the base of the cliff."

"What kind of boat? Will it float?"

Marianne screwed her eyes shut and shook her head. "I didn't see the boat. When we were at the cave, Dirk ran in and shouted that he could see one. I never saw it; I was distracted by the bananas."

"But what else did he say?"

"Nothing. We got distracted by the bananas and never got a chance to properly look at it."

There was a silence, broken only by the sound of wind whistling around the rocks. Inge stared at Marianne a moment, then looked down the cliff to where the cave was.

"We have to check out that boat."

"No way, going there would be suicide. Didn't you hear how all the other crabs lined up along the beach? You saw them all chasing us last time, what if they are all still there waiting for us to go back and have another trap there waiting for us? Plus, we don't even know what condition the boat would be in. It might end up being just another piece of bait."

Inge turned back to Marianne. "So, you're voting option A. Kill Leigh?"

Marianne turned away. She clenched her fists in frustration. How did it come to this? How do you even go about making such choices? This, surely, was not what life was about. Life was about simple choices. About choosing which milk to have in your coffee. Choosing whether to drive yourself to work or take the train. Going out to a movie or to a bar. It should not be choosing between killing someone or risking your own life.

Marianne closed her eyes. What was it her mother always said when she had to make a tough decision? Trust your gut. And what did her gut say? It said she was not capable of killing someone. Not even a crazy, fucked up, rock throwing asshole like Leigh. She took in a deep breath and turned to Inge, hoping she would not regret it.

"OK. We try to get the boat."

20

Leigh strode downhill and did not look back. He had given the girls the most fearsome look he could muster and escaped the scene. They were probably both scared of him now. Good. If they were scared then he would not have to deal with any more crap from them.

Andy. Fuck. He had killed Andy. He was sure of it. Should he feel regret about that? He did not. He was still angry with him. Andy stole Carly and then stole Inge. People like that fucking deserved to die. Leigh was glad he was dead. The truth was clear now. Andy had only been masquerading as his friend. He only wanted to use Leigh. Always ordering Leigh around to take Andy's photo for Andy's glorification and then stealing Leigh's girls. But it was over now. Good.

Leigh stormed onto the beach and sat in the sand. There were no crabs about. Also good. The last thing he needed right now was to deal with those things as well. He crammed his headphones into his ears and thumbed through his phone for the angriest music he could find. He wanted to keep his anger levels high. He did not want to lose it and regret what happened in the ruin.

He picked a nu-metal album from his catalogue. He barely listened to nu-metal anymore. His taste in that style of music had only been a phase. But it worked for him now. He scrunched up his face and nodded his head in time with the beats. Yeah, he thought, I am a badass.

Then he thought about Inge. He did not want her anymore. Andy had spoiled her for him. The thought of kissing her made him feel ill now. How could he put his mouth on hers knowing that Andy might have put his dick there? Yuck. No thanks.

Fucking Andy. He ruins everything.

Leigh sat for a long time, absorbing the anger from the music and staring at the water in front of him. He was so deeply consumed in the rotating destructive thoughts that for a long time he failed to notice the water was clear of crabs. It was only as he was imagining Inge covered with crabs begging for him to save her (which he would not, of course, because she was a traitorous slut and deserved it) that he first noticed the fact.

He stood slowly and pulled the headphones from his ears, scarcely believing they had gone. He walked to the water and peered in. Nothing but white sand whichever way he looked.

He put his phone down and pulled off his shoes. He cast them aside and turned his attention back to the water. He cautiously put his foot in the water. He almost expected the crabs to suddenly rise from under the sand and assault him with their sharp little claws. But nothing happened.

He stepped into the water and stood ankle deep. The waves gently lapped against his shins. The water remained clean and clear of crabs. He wondered where they had gone.

Far ahead, he noticed an object floating in the water. It was difficult to make out as it bobbed up and down. It was orange in colour, and as he focused on the object, he made it out to be a life jacket.

A surge of hope filled him as he searched the ocean for the object's source. But there was nothing. Wherever this life jacket had come from, it had long floated away from its source.

Leigh stood there pondering the life jacket. If he swam out to it, could he use it to swim back to Panama? The idea was illogical, they had been in the boat with Jorge for a long time and there was no way of telling if the tides would take him closer or further away from Panama, but surely there was a chance? He shook his head. Surely it was not possible. But the temptation remained. All he had to do was swim out and grab it.

Leigh looked at the clear sand around his feet and then up at the ruins. He did not fancy spending a night up there under another crab siege. He imagined all those creepy, crawly crabs surrounding them again, this time with them backed up against the cliff. It was something he could not stand going through again. He recalled the horrible ticking sound, the noise the crab claws made when they scratched against the canvas of the tent, and the sight of the cans torn to pieces. He shivered. No, he could not go through another night like that. When the crabs came inland, they were looking for food. And now there was no food, only people. And Leigh had no intention of ending up as the next crab meal.

Leigh looked back to the bobbing life jacket. A means of escape had presented itself. He had to take it.

He walked deeper into the water up to his waist. He turned once more to the ruins and shook his head. If Inge had not been such a slut, he probably would have stayed to protect her. He would have died protecting her. That's how much he loved her. But she had proven she was not worthy of that love. He turned back to the life jacket. He only lived for himself now. He would take the life jacket and escape this hell alone.

Leigh dived forward and began to swim.

21

Marianne poured water into a cloth and began patting down Dirk's skin. She looked up at the sun, shining brilliantly high in the sky above them. She pursed her lips and looked around the ruin.

"We should put one of the tents back up, or at least move Dirk to another spot. We don't want the sun burning him while we're gone."

Marianne continued to pat the wet cloth over Dirk's skin as she waited for a response from her friend, but none came.

"Inge, are you listening to me?"

She turned to see Inge looking down the cliff. Inge held an open palm out, then turned with a grin on her face.

"You wouldn't believe what I just saw," she said. "Crabs. Thousands of them. They just poured out of the cave and into the water. You were right, the cave was a trap."

"And that makes you happy?"

"What?" Inge asked, momentarily confused. She shook her head. "I'm grinning because they *left* the cave. They just came out and went into the ocean. Don't you get it? The boat in the cave is now unguarded."

Marianne bit her lip. Could it be true? She dropped the cloth and stood up.

"Ok, we have to go quickly."

Inge shook her head.

"No, you stay here and look after Dirk. Just keep checking over the side for me. If the boat is worth retrieving and I can't do it on my own, I'll signal for you to come down and help. Otherwise, I'll get the boat out and then help you bring down Dirk."

Marianne nodded, then looked Inge sharply in the eye.

"Ok, but what about Leigh? I don't want you running into him alone down there. God knows what he is capable of right now. He could try to rape you or something."

Inge stared solemnly at her a moment and nodded. She stepped forward and started going through the camping gear Jorge had provided. She dug into the cookware, sorting through the various implements before pulling a carving knife out. It had a twelve-inch blade. They had used it to cut potatoes the night before.

"I'll take this," she said, brandishing it like a sword.

Marianne bit her lip and nodded.

Before another word was said, Inge stepped out of the ruins and started walking downhill. She moved quickly and deliberately to avoid saying awkward goodbyes. Marianne watched her wend her way down.

"Good luck," she said meekly.

22

The agonising pain was the first thing Andy became aware of.

It seared at his back and throbbed in his head. He let out an involuntary cry. His mouth was painfully dry. He was lying awkwardly on his back. He looked up and the sun glared in his eyes. He shaded his face with one hand and he squinted to see a cliff face rise up on one side of his body, and empty space drop away on the other. He felt disoriented, and for a long moment he had no idea where he was.

Then it hit him like an electric shock. The fight with Leigh. The fall.

For a second he panicked, thinking he had fallen all the way down, but then he noticed the clifftop was not far above him. He had not fallen the full distance. He must have landed on a ledge. It was uncomfortable, and he seemed to be lying on some sort of protuberance.

He tried to raise himself to sit. Visceral pain roared through his body and his vision darkened. He relaxed back down and took a few deep breaths.

Ok, he thought, let's just take this easy for now. He waited for his vision to clear once more. He looked about. The ledge he was on was quite narrow. The cliff dropped away on one side barely a foot away from his left side. To his right, the cliff wall was just out of arm's length away. At the intersection of the cliff and the ledge, a small crab stood watching him. It had a grey-blue shell, and its oval eyes swivelled as it examined him. It had one normal sized claw. The second claw was almost as big as its carapace.

"Fuck off," Andy yelled at it. The crab was unmoved.

He felt around the ledge around him. He found a small rock and threw it at the crab. It scuttled sideways, moving close to Andy's right leg. He decided to kick it away. He focused on the crab and struck.

Nothing happened. His foot did not move.

He frowned. He tried again. Nothing.

Suddenly he felt panic rising inside. Something was wrong. Very wrong.

Andy took a deep breath and focused. He willed his foot to move. Nothing. Next, he tried something simpler. He tried to wiggle his toes. He forced his head up, working through the pain so he could see his toes clearly. He willed his toes to move. Nothing happened.

Andy began to despair. Then the crab moved. Helplessly, he watched the crab walk close to him.

"Get away," Andy yelled at it. "Fuck off."

The crab scuttled close. Its eyestalks swivelled as it regarded him. It crept closer still, getting braver with each sideways step. The crab reached Andy's leg and climbed up. Andy felt nothing. The crab's eyes continued to swivel about. It hefted its large claw forward and pinched Andy's flesh. Andy saw the skin gripped between the crab's claw pulled white and taut by the mean little bugger. But he felt nothing.

He swore and started feeling around for another rock to throw at it. One came to hand, and he turned to throw, only to find it was no longer on his legs. Desperately he looked around, finally spying it regarding him from the edge of the ledge. For a moment Andy looked at it, wondering why the crab had moved on after pinching him so. Then the crab disappeared from sight, crawling spider-like down the cliff face.

Andy stared at the spot a moment before laying his head back and tried to relax. He was in a fix and he knew it. The ledge was in a tricky spot. Even if he could move, any attempt to climb back up would be too precarious to risk. But he could not even wiggle his toes. He could not imagine the others mounting a rescue either. It was far too dangerous. He would have to wait for them to get back to Bocas Town and arrange some sort of professional rescue. He might be stuck here for days.

He tried not to think about it. He did not want to think about spending days up here alone on the edge of a cliff waiting for a rescue. He turned his mind to Leigh. God, Leigh had really lost his nut this time. He wished Leigh could just be normal with girls. It should not have to be like this. Leigh had always been weird around women he liked, and the older he got the worse he was. Despite all the advice Andy and others gave him, Leigh just kept going the same way about it, and it never ended well.

He supposed this time was genuinely the end of their twenty-odd year friendship. How could it go on after this? Andy certainly was not going to put in the hard yards this time, not after Leigh had pushed him over a cliff. But had Leigh heard the warning and pushed him over deliberately? That was the real question here. He thought back to Leigh's face, screwed up in anger. Could he have been so blind with rage that he did not hear?

No, Andy thought, that should not matter. Andy dumped Carly for Leigh. Andy was the one always cleaning up after Leigh acted out, making excuses to explain his behaviour. He even made excuses for him after the Angela incident, and he was pretty sure Leigh was at fault there. Andy had been the one who made all the effort to keep their friendship going. For everything Andy had done, look at where it had landed him. On a ledge with a potentially broken spine.

"Hey," a female voice called from above him.

Andy blinked the tears from his eyes and focused on the head that had appeared at the top of the cliff.

"Marianne," he exclaimed.

"Are you ok down there?"

"No. I have a lot of pain. I think I may have a broken back. I can't move or feel my body from the waist down."

For a long moment Marianne stared at him and said nothing.

"Where are the others?" Andy asked to break the silence.

"Leigh stormed off after the fight. I haven't seen him in a while. Inge went down to check out the boat."

"What boat?"

"Dirk saw a boat in the cave, but we never checked it out because we saw the bananas, so now Inge has gone to see if it's usable. We were hoping to get off the island." Marianne looked behind her, and as she turned back, Andy could see she was biting her lip. "Listen, I know Leigh's your friend and all but I have to ask. If Inge ran into him down there, he wouldn't do anything to her, would he?"

"He's never physically hurt a girl he liked."

Well actually, Andy thought, maybe once, if the rumour was to be believed. Best not mention that though. The was too much to worry about as it was. He swallowed. His mouth was dry and uncomfortable. "Hey, I'm really thirsty down here. Do you think you could toss down a bottle of water for me? And some painkillers if we have any?"

Marianne's head disappeared and shortly later she returned with a bottle of water and some headache tablets.

"It's all we have," she explained.

"It's okay," he said.

She dropped them one at a time to Andy. He caught the bottle in front of his face. The packet of tablets was noticeably lighter, and as it tumbled, the wind took it away from him. Thankfully, the tablets landed on the ledge, but like the crab from earlier, they were just outside of Andy's reach.

"Sorry," Marianne called.

Andy acknowledged the apology with a wave of his hand. He stretched out, wincing in pain as he tried desperately to reach the small packet. It could not have been more than an inch away, yet it may as well have been a mile for all the good it did him. He tried using the water bottle as an extension of his arm, but rather than drag the packet closer, he only succeeded in pushing it farther away.

He cursed. He was more useless than a turtle stuck on its back. Eventually the agony that laced his body became too much to bear and he ceased his efforts. They were only headache tablets. What good would they do for someone with a broken back anyway?

He looked back up the cliff. Marianne had gone. He thanked her for that. She had left him with some dignity by not watching his failed struggle to get a small packet an inch out of reach. He forced himself to semi-sit and drank from the bottle. It was painful, but he needed the drink, and his body thanked him when he lay back down afterwards.

Then Andy began to fret. What if it really was a broken back? He focused on his toes and tried to wiggle them once more. Still nothing. He slumped back. He tried to recall what he knew about broken backs. Was it possible to recover from one and walk again? He did not know. He was sure he had seen a movie about a guy who was told he would never walk again. It was one of those inspirational true stories, where the main character overcomes extreme adversity. He could remember the uplifting music as the guy walked again at the end of the movie, but, dammit, did he have a broken back? The detail did not seem important at the time but could not matter more to Andy right now.

Andy's head swam. He could not imagine a life where he could not walk again. Everything would be so different. So hard. He had never known someone in a wheelchair before, but everything he had seen made it look like their life was hard. His life would be significantly altered. The world was not built for people in wheelchairs to openly access everything. And it was not just about mobility either. The way they were viewed by the rest of the world was different too. If he ever got out of here, that is.

Then a thought struck him.

"Marianne," he called. He waited a moment then called again. "Marianne, I need you."

Her head appeared at the top of the cliff once more.

"Marianne, I need you to do something for me. I want you to go into my bag and get my camera. I want you to take photos of me."

Her face screwed up like a scrunched ball of paper. "What?"

"Hear me out," he pleaded. "I want photos of me, like this. Then I want you to make a video. Film the area at the top where we scuffled and show where I fell and show me lying here. Don't mention Leigh by name, just show the area so my audience can understand what happened to me."

"Your audience?" For a moment she looked completely bewildered. "Let me get this straight, you are stuck down there and maybe paralysed for life and all you are thinking about is what to post on social media?"

Andy's lip quivered and his voice was unsteady. "I know what you must be thinking. You must think I'm some self-absorbed moron who is seeing this as content that will get sympathy views and likes. It's not like that. It's just… social media is my life. I paid for this trip with the money I earned from doing it. I've worked so hard to get to where I am, and I'm not just going to give it away because of this. So, my story changes. I won't be the party boy who has the life and adventures everyone follows to see and envy. My story becomes something else. A guy adjusting to life after a traumatic event. I still have a story to tell. I can still be someone worth following."

Marianne looked down at him sadly.

"Look," he said, "you don't have to understand or agree with me about this. I won't ask that of you. I only ask you do this, as a friend. Could you take the photos and make the video? Please?"

She stared a long time and nodded.

Andy heaved a sigh of relief. He lay back. He could still do it, he told himself. He could still be an influencer. He might turn over his audience completely and need to find a whole new set of followers, but he could do it. He could still live his dream.

He just needed to get off this Godforsaken island first.

23

Inge was acting braver than she felt.

The absolute last thing she had wanted to do right now was go off on her own. She gripped the hilt of the knife so tightly her knuckles turned white with the strain. Her eyes darted constantly about, despite the large plain of open space around her. The confrontation at the ruins had spooked her to the core in ways she had never felt before. Leigh was clearly unhinged, and that meant he could be dangerous and unpredictable. She needed to stay on guard.

But what alternative had she other than to leave the ruin? Ultimately, it had come down to choosing between the lesser of two fears. The crabs were creepy, but Leigh was creepier. How did he already have it in his head that he loved her? He barely knew her. Added to that, if Inge had pieced together the facts yelled during the argument correctly, Leigh had a history of this sort of behaviour, which just made it worse. When it came down to it, Inge saw only two options; either to face the crabs for a way off the island, or face Leigh.

Inge looked down at the nick she had received from the rock Leigh had thrown. It stung as she walked. The choice was clear for her. She would rather face the crabs ninety-nine times out of a hundred than spend any more time with Leigh. She felt the blade of her knife, savouring the cold strength of it. She chose facing the crabs because she knew if she ran into Leigh again, one or both of their lives would be changed irrevocably.

Thankfully, there was no sign of Leigh anywhere. As she stepped onto the beach, she did notice something blue in the sand not far away. She glanced up and down the beach to ensure there was no place Leigh could conceal himself to ambush her, but she failed to spot anything of significance. As she closed in, she could see it was Leigh's t-shirt and shoes lying abandoned on the beach. In the sand next to them was his phone and earbud headphones. She stared at them suspiciously.

Footprints led away from the shoes to the water's edge and disappeared. She looked out to the water, suddenly hopeful the problem she had had been solved by other means, but then she spotted him. He was swimming away from the island, his strong strokes cutting through the water easily. She frowned at the curious turn of events, and studied the water before her. It was curiously clear of crabs. She felt like sneering at the irony. The one time the water was clear and the last thing she wanted was to swim. Not with that madman out there.

Inge turned and walked swiftly along the beach. She wanted to get to the cave quickly and study the boat. There was haste to her mission now. Leigh could turn and spot her at any moment. He could come ashore and follow her to the cave, trapping her. The last thing she wanted was to be backed up into a cave with him. She clenched the knife tightly.

She decided to quicken her pace, almost jogging, as she glanced continually over her shoulder to where Leigh swam. Perhaps it was an irrational fear, perhaps Leigh would calm down and come to his senses, but a dreaded fear nagged at her. She glanced up the side of the cliff, hopeful to see the outline of Marianne at the top, as though her image would be a magical talisman that could provide her with the strength and courage she would need if Leigh did spot and follow her. But Marianne was nowhere to be seen.

Inge could see the cave ahead. She slowed her pace and caught her breath. A look out to sea told her Leigh was still swimming, and his splashing form was quite distant now. She took a couple of deep breaths. She could not be certain whether or not he had spotted her, but he was far enough away that she felt safe for now.

Inge glanced up at the cliff face for the bananas. She was wary not to fall for the same trap, but the point was moot as she saw no sign of the 'bait'.

She turned her eyes cave-ward. She could see very little beyond the mouth, as though a thick dark fabric was draped down to prevent her from seeing inside. She edged forward, studying the small pock marks the army of crabs had left in the sand. There were millions of them. The sand was more punctured than her grandmother's ancient pincushion. She shivered. She had not seen so many crabs in one place like this before. Individually, they were nothing to worry about. She had picked one up easily last night. But in numbers like this....

Suddenly Leigh no longer seemed the most dangerous thing she could encounter down here.

She looked up the cliff wall for her magical talisman. There was no sign of Marianne. She frowned, turning back to the cave. With one more nervous glance towards the sea, she stepped forward to the cave entrance.

The cave was dim inside, and she stood on the threshold a moment, waiting for her eyes to adjust. On the left was two large rocks, just by the entrance. She eyed them cautiously, wary they may be a good place for a crab to hide. On her right was the boat. She shuffled quickly to it. It was a simple, wooden rowboat that may have once served as an emergency boat for a ship. There was enough room to fit four comfortably on the two benches that served as seats. Its paint was old and faded, but the timbers of the hull still looked relatively solid. The hull was filled with a couple of inches of sand.

She walked slowly around the boat, occasionally giving it a hefty whack to ensure it was still strong. Slowly, she began nodding her head. It would do. This should float. The only problem would be the bench seats. They would not be able to lie Dirk down comfortably in the boat, but at least they could get away.

Then Inge noticed a bigger issue with the plan. There was only one oar in the boat. With only one oar, they would flounder, succeeding only in turning in circles on the water. Inge swore softly and stared into the darker depths of the cave. They needed the second oar. There was no point pushing out to sea with no means of propelling the boat away from the island. They could just be washed back ashore where Leigh and the crabs awaited them.

She then remembered Marianne had brought a torch. Marianne was safety conscious, and always packed ordinary things that most people would not think of for the simple reason that you never knew when you might need it. The first aid kit. Matches. A pocket knife with the full complement of features. And, of course, a torch.

Inge walked back out of the cave and looked up the cliff face. Her eyes needed a moment to readjust to the light, and she needed to squint for a minute. She waited, but no sign of Marianne appeared. For a moment she considered calling out for Marianne. It seemed risky; the sound was more likely to echo off the cliffs and be heard by Leigh than Marianne.

She looked out to the sea. She spotted Leigh quickly. He was no longer splashing amongst the waves, but rather he appeared to be standing up with the water only knee high about him. He appeared to be looking about. Inge frowned. He was quite a way out, what on earth could he be standing on?

Inge suddenly realised she may be exposed to being spotted by him, and backed back into the cave behind her. The shadow of the cave passed over her, and she stood there a moment to watch what Leigh would do. He stood a full minute doing nothing. She was staring at him intently when suddenly she heard a sound behind her.

She jumped and turned, holding the knife before her. It had only been a slight sound, like a stone falling, but it made her wary. She stepped cautiously forwards, her nerves suddenly strained and her muscles taut. She scanned the darkness for movement, but there she saw nothing.

She took two more steps forward. The knife was steady in her hand, poised and ready to strike. She tried to tell herself it was nothing. It was only a small sound, there surely was no danger here…

A crab scuttled out of the darkness.

She jumped at the sudden movement. The crab was only a foot across and scampered quickly across the sand past her. She watched it go. It held its claws high as it ran, clacking them in alarm as it went.

Inge let out a breath slowly. She, too, was letting herself get spooked too easily by the crabs. They had not bothered her at first, but last night when they came ashore it had been a little disconcerting. Then the story of the 'trap' that had snared Dirk got her genuinely worried. Andy seemed unphased, and she found herself drawing strength from his fearlessness of the situation. It was especially helpful when Marianne was fretting so restlessly the previous night. It was why she left the tent and sat with Andy. She just could not stand it in the tent. She loved Marianne, but by God, sometimes she required the patience of a saint to be with. Dirk, in many ways, was that saint, and that is why they were so perfect for each other.

But now she too was getting jumpy around the crabs. She wished Andy was here with her now.

With the crab gone, Inge turned back to the dark depths of the cave. No doubt it was that crab which had made the noise. She was certain she was alone now. She took a deep breath and stepped further into the depths of the cave. She needed to find that oar.

24

Leigh's strong strokes drove him through the warm water at pace.

He had always been told he was a natural swimmer. His parents had made swimming lessons a priority from an early age, and he took to water as though he was born for it. His naturally broad shoulders and smooth technique saw him slice through the water with natural ease. He had won many ribbons at a young age for his swimming, but come puberty he lost his zest for it and abandoned all forms of competitive swimming.

He may have been out of practice, but Leigh was still a strong swimmer. He cut through the water as cleanly as he always had, pushing through the waves with his muscular shoulders and zeroing in quickly on the life jacket he had spotted.

There were no doubts in Leigh's mind anymore. He knew he was right to escape, and to escape alone. In his mind, he toyed briefly with the idea he could still reconcile with Inge. It was possible. With Andy technically out of the picture, surely there was a way he could bring her around to seeing the light? But did he still want her?

No, he decided. No, he did not. Once Andy had been in her, she was more spoiled to him than fruit that had been left under the boiling sun for a week. He could not touch her without thinking about Andy. The fantasy of her was ruined.

Leigh swam on, focused on his target, when his hands struck sand. He pulled up, and as he shifted his body into an upright position in the water, his feet touched sand and he realised that he could stand up. Confused, he stood and looked about. The island was far behind him, yet he seemed to have hit a sandbar of some sort. He walked forwards, rising out of the water until it was little more than knee high. He stopped and looked around.

The water was clear and he could see the sandbar stretched a long way to both his left and right. It seemed strange and unnatural to him for the sand to form like this around the island. He stood a moment and thought. He remembered the strange course Jorge had taken to the island. The great curving S shapes he had cut through the water. Evidently Jorge was aware of the sandbar, but how many S shapes had Jorge made? He squinted at the sea ahead. Jorge had made many turns. Did that mean there were more sandbars like this ahead of Leigh?

He shook his head. He was no expert in the matter, but multiple long sandbars around an island like this were certainly not a naturally occurring phenomena. Surely, they were man made. But to serve what purpose? To keep people from the island? Leigh scratched his head. He guessed it could theoretically stop boats from making landfall unless they knew the route through them, but then wouldn't unknowing boats get beached on the sandbars and need rescuing?

And then there was the question of maintenance. Again, he was no expert, but surely the coming and going of the tides would ebb away the sandbars over time? As a child he could recall building sandcastles and trenches in sand at the beach only to watch them wash away when the waves came in. A few waves and you would never know Leigh's castle with deep moats had ever been there. Using the same theory, how was it these sandbars stayed?

Suddenly something brushed his foot. He jumped, clouding the water with sand around him. His heartrate leapt as he found himself looking at the water around him. He had forgotten the crabs for a moment, and only now he realised how vulnerable he was standing there. He watched the sand on the water glitter and settle, like a snow globe that had been recently shaken.

Then another thought struck him. What if a boat did approach the island and maroon itself there? The passengers would be stuck there for hours. What purpose would these underwater dunes have by stranding people that could not be better served by a warning sign on the island?

Unless these sandbars were not made by men to keep people away.

What if their exact purpose was *to* strand boats? Who would stand the most to gain by that?

As if in answer to Leigh's unvoiced question, a series of bubbles burst as they reached the surface of the water nearby. He looked down to see the depths around him were alive with movement as hordes of grey crabs half crawled, half glided across the sand below. There were thousands of them, and they were all converging on one point. They were converging on Leigh.

A dreaded thought entered his mind. Did the crabs build these sandbars to trap boats and people here deliberately? To trap… food? The idea repulsed Leigh, and seemed too farfetched to be real, yet somehow, he knew it had to be true. He could see it in his mind. A crew working restlessly trying to free their boat while hordes of murderous crabs clambered aboard with the intent to kill. The very image of it gave him chills. Despite how fanciful it seemed it was the only logical reason for the sandbars to exist.

But there was no time to think; Leigh needed to move before the crabs reached him. His eyes flicked over to his original target: the life jacket. For a moment he considered leaping in that direction and swimming towards it, but the thought of more sandbars ahead stopped him. He could not know how many more were out there, but surely swimming from one to another was too fraught with danger. He could reach the next sandbar only to find them already waiting for him. Going back would be safer. At least on the island he would be able to see all around and defend himself.

He made a snap decision, and leapt into the water. He splashed around clumsily at first. The water was too shallow and he kicked and pushed against the sand, struggling to get momentum. His foot hit something hard, sparking panic and he floundered a minute. A sharp pain scoured his foot and he kicked hard to push his body out over deeper water. As he got into deeper water, he paused a moment and looked down into the water. He could see shadows moving swiftly along the sea floor below him.

He swivelled to look back at where he had been. The sandbar was covered with grey, rock-like shapes. They were streaming over it like ants on a nest. There was no recourse now, he had to swim back to the island.

Leigh swore and turned. He shifted his weight in the water and began to swim freestyle towards the island. He opened his eyes and looked down. The shapes of the crabs were gliding on the sea floor below him. They, too, were heading to the island, and Leigh realised suddenly he was in a race.

With panic fraying the last rational threads of his mind, Leigh was unable to relax into a smooth and quick stroke. His legs and arms were all out of time with each other, and as Leigh took his next breath, he looked up towards the island. He seemed no closer to land than he had been when he was on the sandbar.

He sensed, more than saw, the monstrous dark shadows that skimmed the sand below. Despite their ungainly shapes, the crabs moved with an elegance under the water, cutting a smooth and fast sideways trajectory towards the beach.

Leigh clenched his teeth and pushed harder. The muscles across his shoulders and down his legs began to ache, and for the first time in a long time, he regretted not persisting with swimming. All the time he spent in the gym had built him muscles not stamina. He was not used to the sustained effort and was beginning to fatigue. The breaths he gulped at greedily between strokes began feeling inadequate. He wanted to stop and rest, but the shadows of the monstrous little predators drove him on.

The sand floor then began rising towards him. He thought it was an illusion at first, and took a moment between strokes to look up towards the island. The beach was up in front of him. He had closed on it quicker than he had thought. He put his head back under and pushed on. Claw-like shapes loomed out of the depths and reached towards him. Leigh kicked his feet harder as they closed and felt his skin tingle in anticipation of the claw snips to come.

The sand was rising fast and soon Leigh would be forced to stand up. It was then Leigh realised the futility of his flight. Walking through water was slow and laborious. There was no way he could wade through the water quickly enough to escape his chasers. The crabs moved far too quickly under the water for him to get away. Soon the little fiends would be climbing all over him, pinching and scratching him with their claws and dragging him under the water with their weight. For a moment Leigh thought of turning and heading back out and floating in a deep part of the water far from their reach. But it was an unrealistic plan; he could not float out there forever on his own.

Leigh pushed on but the water grew shallow fast. His hand came into contact with sand and dug in. The water was alive with shapes and movement. This is it, thought Leigh, they have me. He twisted his body around to sit with his back to the beach. If this was his fate, he wanted to face it, not have it drag him down from behind.

He sat, the water sitting just above his nipples. The crabs loomed menacingly before him in the water, their presence as haunting as the grim reaper himself. The reflections of the water danced across their carapaces as they suddenly all became still.

Leigh watched a moment, wondering why they waited to strike.

"Come on, what are you waiting for? Do it," Leigh yelled.

Suddenly water surged with bubbles and sand. Leigh closed his eyes, bracing for the claws to pinch his skin and legs to rake his flesh. But nothing happened, and slowly he opened his eyes to see the settling waters around him. Confused, he looked about. The monstrous crabs had gone. He blinked, disbelieving.

Slowly, Leigh backed out of the water and up onto the beach. He collapsed onto his bottom into the sand as he gulped at mouthfuls of air. What had just happened? The crabs just had him, dead to rights, and instead of killing him they had just darted away as if in a great hurry. What had been the big emergency?

Leigh glanced along the beach in confusion. He started to think again about his theory of the traps. Andy had laughed at him. Well fuck Andy. He probably laughed as he fucked Inge too. Well Andy was wrong and Leigh was right. The bananas on the cliff were a trap, and so were the sandbars. The crabs had meticulously built, and maintained, the sandbars out in the water as traps for boats with one intention: to hunt and kill humans.

Leigh shook his head. These crabs were something else. They were smart, and they were killers. But why had they let him go?

Leigh looked back up the beach and saw the horde emerging from the water. They were returning to the cave. Leigh frowned. What could possibly be so urgent at the cave that would drive them all away from their prey right when it had him?

25

Marianne pressed the large red square on the screen to end the recording before heaving a great sigh. It was done. She had filmed Andy's damn video explaining the scuffle and fall. She could barely believe Andy had wanted the story preserved, nor did she like that her re-telling of events would be posted online for many people to view and hear. She had always been subconscious about her accent and her weak English grammar, but that was not what had bothered her most about doing the video. What bothered her most was repeating the things Leigh had said and done. It disgusted her to her core.

She switched the device off and tucked it into a pocket in Andy's bag. She had not held her tongue like Andy had asked. She had given the whole story, warts and all. From Leigh's sick jealous obsession, his venomous and grotesque insults, to his deliberate push of Andy over the cliff. She told it all. Leigh did not deserve to be let off after what he had done.

She walked over to the edge to notify Andy his video was done, but as she shouted down to him, she realised he had once more passed out. A mere ten minutes ago, he had been giving her the thumbs up in a series of photos. She shook her head and pulled away from the cliff.

She made her way to the other cliff edge that stood over the beach and cave. She had promised Inge she would keep a regular eye on things, but the video from Andy had distracted her. She scanned the beach for a moment, looking for any sign of Inge, but she saw nothing. There was not a single soul on the beach as far as she could tell.

Marianne pulled away from the edge and decided she needed to attend to Dirk. The sun was high above and blazing on him now. Remembering how liberally Dirk always applied sunscreen, she knew she would have to set up a tent to move him undercover. He burnt easily, and the last thing his body needed was to battle sunburn on top of his wounds.

As she moved towards him, though, she was stopped short by something strange. At first, she thought someone had placed a stone on his chest, but at the sound of her footsteps, the 'stone' rose on spindly legs to face her. Marianne grimaced and her step faltered as she got closer. She could not let it stay there, but the best she could come up with was waving her hand ineffectually at it.

"Shoo," she said. The crab regarded her silently with its oval eyes.

Marianne reached into a pack and pulled out a small towel. She twisted it around, and then danced around and flicked the towel at the crab. "Shoo," she cried again. "Get away from him."

The crab was unmoved, clearly unimpressed by her histrionics. Then the edge of the towel flicked the crab. It reared up onto its legs and raised its claws. "Ha," Marianne whooped with success as she danced on her toes like a boxer in the ring. "You want some more of that?"

She flicked the towel again, this time hitting the crab flush on the body. The crab was dashed aside, landing in the dirt before scuttling away between a gap between two stones of the wall of the ruin.

She let out another whoop of joy, celebrating the moment as though she had just won the boxing world heavyweight championship. Casting the towel aside, she cleaned Dirk's skin with a damp cloth and started applying the sunscreen to his exposed skin. She would still need to assemble the tent, but that should protect him for now.

Marianne then checked over the edge for Inge again. There was nobody below her at the cave, but she spied a figure sitting on the beach some distance away from her. The figure was too far away to see who it was. She waved at it, but from the figure there was no response.

Pulling back from the edge, Marianne made her way to the tent. They had not packed it properly earlier, but it should just be a simple matter for her to unfold it, raise it, clip the poles in place and peg it to the ground.

She turned over the first flap of fabric, exposing a crab which had been nestling in the folds. It rose up on its legs and snapped its claws aggressively. Despite herself, Marianne let out a small squeal and tumbled backwards to land on her rump. She hated animals at the best of times, but having them jump out and act aggressively was a whole new level. She cursed the creature and looked around for the towel. She was sure she had dropped it near Dirk, yet it was nowhere to be seen. Movement caught her eye, and she saw the towel moving around the corner of the doorway of the ruin.

"What the hell?" she murmured to herself. She got to her feet and followed the towel. As she got closer, she could see a bluish-grey crab had the towel clutched in its claws and was dragging it away. She backed slowly back into the ruin.

When she turned back around, more crabs had appeared in the ruin. They regarded her with oval eyes on raised stalks. Two stood by the edge where only moments before she had crouched to look over the edge for Inge. Another had appeared in the opposite corner, and two more had been crawling across the centre of the ruins when she turned.

Marianne glanced at Dirk. Leigh's 'trap to catch food' theory came to mind again. Was it Dirk's body that was drawing them here? She shivered at the memory of how Leigh had described it. The bananas were bait intended to trap one of them. Were they now coming here for their food? An uninvited shiver ran down her spine. Irrational panic threatened to overwhelm her as she ran across to Dirk to check his pulse, fearing the appearance of the crabs as a sign that he may have passed and that they had come to collect their fodder.

She placed her fingers against his neck. From the corner of her eye, she caught more movement, but she resisted the urge to look and focused on finding a pulse. It was faint, but it was there. She heaved a sigh of relief. But as she looked around, more crabs began to appear. They were not coming because he had passed, they were coming to claim their prize: meat they had lured into their trap at the cave.

Her eyes widened as they darted from one crab to the next. At least ten more had entered the ruins since she had crouched to check Dirk's pulse. They were not supposed to be coming yet. Not until dusk. Dusk was at least three hours away.

Marianne felt her heartrate rise and her breathing became ragged. She glanced to where Inge had gone, hoping eagerly for the sight of her friend returning, but there was none. With Dirk and Andy incapacitated, she felt dreadfully and utterly alone.

Marianne remembered how as a child she was told to be confident around dogs. "You have to act brave, even when you are not," her parents said. "Dogs can smell fear."

As a child, she never knew if that was true or not, but she always acted brave around dogs when she was inwardly cringing and craving to run away. But she had also been cynical of the smell fear theory. How could fear even have a smell? It had been years later when the subject had come up in a drunken discussion at a bar she was told by a would be suitor that fear itself did not have a smell, but the body released pheromones that a dog would pick up on. In a way, dogs could indeed smell 'fear'.

Marianne eyed the crabs in the clearing and wondered if they, like dogs, could detect and understand her emotional state. Perhaps that was why they were coming now. They knew she was afraid and potentially irrational. They had marked her as a weak link in the group, and now that she was isolated from the others, they were moving in.

Her skin crawled at the idea and she shook her head frenetically, as though the very act would shake the dreaded idea from her mind. But the thought remained when she stopped and once again looked across the ruins at the crabs who all stood still, watching her with those cold, dark oval eyes they had.

She wanted to scream. Her hands were shaking and she could not control them. Dogs. Cats. Horses. Lizards. Birds. Mice. Bats. Even cute animals like guinea pigs. And now crabs. She hated them all. She did not want them near her. But she knew she could not let the fear get the best of her. Not if she wanted to protect Dirk.

Marianne rose to her feet on unsteady legs. She looked around desperately for a weapon when she noticed the wood pile. She smiled. She had been a decent hockey player in high school. She darted across to the pile, throwing branches and planks left and right as she tried to find something usable. She settled on a long, thin knobbly stick that widened at one end. It was only half the length of a hockey stick, but it was the easiest to hold with two hands.

Hefting the stick in front of her like Arthur holding Excalibur, Marianne suddenly felt renewed strength rising inside her. The crab that had hidden amongst the folds of the tent and surprised and menaced her earlier still stood proudly on the canvas watching her. She pointed her stick out in challenge, then broke into a run towards it. Sensing the fight coming, the crab raised its claws high. Marianne swung her stick and felt the satisfying clunk as the stick smashed the crab's bony carapace. It had not been a clean hit, but it was enough to send the little monster hurtling away minus two legs.

"Ha," Marianne screamed, "how did you like that?"

There was only silence in the ruins as the other crabs stood motionless, watching her with unblinking eyes. Despite the sudden surge of adrenaline she had from picking her weapon and hitting the crab, she was still disturbed by the scene around her.

Remembering her primary task, Marianne dropped the stick and stepped over the tent. It was a simple design. The tent was square shaped, with the poles curving from one corner to the opposite, crossing over in the middle in a way that if viewed from above would look like an x in a box. The poles remained in the sleeves of the tent fabric, she just needed to raise and attach the poles to the rings on the base by bending them and peg the tent down. She lifted the poles to give the tent form. She struggled with the first pole a moment, having to push hard to bend it and guide it into the ring. She held the tent upright and walked to the opposite corner to put the next pole in place. From the corners of her eyes, she caught movement around her. More crabs were entering the ruin. She did her best to focus on the job at hand and ignore them.

She forced the second pole in place. She stood, aware crabs were creeping towards both her and the prostrate form of Dirk, closing with each passing second. She felt her heartrate rising once more. The tent wobbled, and Marianne wished someone else was around to hold the tent upright while she fixed the remaining two poles in place.

She leaned forward, picking up the next pole while trying to hold the tent upright at the same time. For a second it keeled over towards where she was squatting, but she raised the next pole in place just in time to prevent it from falling altogether.

More movement caught her eyes and she realised the crabs were entering the ruins in bigger numbers now. She tried not to look their way, afraid of what she might see. She forced the pole to bend, but as she went to push the end of the pole into the ring, she realised her hands were shaking considerably.

"Come on," she willed herself. Twice she pushed the pole down, but missed the ring altogether. She willed herself not to look at how many crabs had come into the clearing. She sensed them all around her. She wished she still had the stick with her so maybe she could whack a few and keep them at bay, but resorting to the stick would mean dropping the tent, and dropping the tent now would see it collapse altogether. She had no intentions of starting over.

She closed her eyes a moment and took a deep breath to compose herself. She needed to get the tent up and Dirk inside. Once erected, they could hide inside like the night previous. The little monsters could scratch and climb the canvas all they wanted, but they could not get in.

Marianne opened her eyes and focused on the ring once more. Her hands still shook, but she willed them still. She pushed the pole down, bending it harder as she did so, forcing it into the ring at last.

She heaved a sigh of relief and straightened up. One more pole to go. In her momentary relief, Marianne forgot herself and glanced around the ruin. There were crabs all about her. There must have been at least fifty in the ruins now, with more spindly legs and stalk-raised eyes appearing over the bricks of the ruins with each passing second.

Fighting down rising panic, Marianne cautiously moved to the opposite side of the tent to place the last pole in place, careful not to let the tent collapse. She glanced towards Dirk to see crabs cautiously closing in on his still form. Some were the size of dinner plates.

She grabbed the pole and bent it down towards the final ring. Her hands were shaking wildly. She placed her foot next to the ring to hold it in place as she used both hands to guide the pole in. The last pole was always the hardest to place at the best of times, requiring the most force of all the poles to bend down and guide in, but it was far worse when your hands shook like a plate of jelly in an earthquake. She stabbed the pole down once, hitting her foot. She winced, but was privately glad she was wearing shoes. The last thing she needed right now was to open her foot up with welts.

The second time she guided it down slower. Despite the shakiness of her hands, she got the pole in place. She straightened and looked at her shaking hands. She could do nothing to control or steady them. Around her, the crabs were starting to swarm. She looked again at their cold, oval eyes. She was certain of it now; they could smell fear. It was why they came now in such numbers. She clenched her shaking hands into fists.

"Fuck you," she screamed. She still needed time to peg the tent into the ground and attach the flysheet. But as she looked at the crabs encroaching on Dirk's body, she knew it was time she could not afford to take. Those things could wait, she needed to get Dirk to safety now.

She surged forwards to her stick, kicking a nearby crab away and picking up her weapon in the blink of an eye. She stepped towards Dirk, swinging the stick like a scythe to cut down any crabs that dared cross her path. Clearing a space, she again dropped the stick and hooked her arms under Dirk's armpits. Through gritted teeth she dragged Dirk to the tent. She unzipped the door and pulled him inside before zipping the tent shut behind her.

Safe at last, Marianne dropped to her knees and allowed herself a moment to catch her breath. Slowly, the shakes disappeared from her hands, and she again checked Dirk's pulse. She knew she did not have to check as regularly as she did, but as long as she felt that soft pulse still there, she had hope.

The soft scratching of claws on canvas started to sound about her. Marianne looked about her at the evil shadows of the crabs as they clambered against the tent. They had totally surrounded the tent, just as they had done the night previous. She checked the tent zipper, making sure it was secure and out of their reach.

She swallowed, realising suddenly how thirsty she was. She looked about, cursing herself for not having the foresight to throw some water bottles into the tent first. The crabs were all around now, she was not leaving this fortress unless forced.

She lay her hand on Dirk's chest. At least they were safe for now. She fretted for Inge. She could not go back and check over the cliff for her. Surely Inge would come back if she did not see Marianne looking down? But then, what would happen if Inge did come back? How would she get through the crabs to the tent to join them?

As if in answer to the unasked question, the sound of scrabbling began to fade. Marianne looked about her as the macabre shapes withdrew from the tent and silence descended across the clearing.

Marianne remained motionless, barely believing the crabs had gone. Slowly, she crept forward and unzipped the door a crack to peer out. The ruins were clear. There was not a crab in sight.

Marianne dropped her head into her hands. She wanted to weep, but she knew it was not over. The crabs would be back at night, she just knew it. This was only a temporary reprieve. Something had drawn them away, but they would be back. It was as sure as the sun setting tonight.

At least now she could get water and check on Inge. She could finish setting up the tent, too. Maybe she could even set up for the night ahead. She could get the fire ready. Set up the bags again.

Suddenly Dirk moaned. Marianne turned to see Dirk's body shudder and for him to kick his leg out violently. A fresh red patch had begun forming on the bandage that covered Dirk's wound.

Marianne's shoulders slumped. "Oh God, please no," she whispered. She knew the signs from the first time. It was hard then, and that was with Andy, Leigh and Inge. Perhaps she could wait until Inge got back?

Dirk shuddered and kicked again.

No, she could not wait. She would need to remove the second crab from his leg on her own.

26

Inge swore in frustration as she tripped over for the third time, landing hard on the packed sand with her knees. It was infernally dark in the cave, and only got worse the deeper she went. She felt like cursing Marianne for failing to be at her post to throw the torch down to her. She may as well have been blind right now, so dark was the cave.

But it was not just the total dark that bothered her. It was the hellish smell as well. There was an overwhelming stench of decay mixed with what she assumed was crab faecal matter. The air was as thick as custard with it, and even when she blocked her nose, the smell still seemed to invade her senses, as though it seeped through her skin and into her being.

Inge grimaced, feeling around the object she had tripped on. The cave had been far deeper than she could have imagined, and finding that damned second oar was proving to be a fruitless exercise. She had already combed a great deal of area, but so wide, deep and dark was the cave she may well have passed it and never known.

She felt the object she had tripped on. It was like a stick, but it was long and smooth. Too thin to be the oar, she followed its curving line with her hand, tracing the shape as she tried to work out what it was. The thing was round in shape, and it ended in a flat, central strut. Other similar sticks curved away from the central strut, like a ribcage. Inge pulled her hand away. No, not *like* a ribcage. This *is* a ribcage.

Inge shivered and turned back to the circle of light that was the cave mouth behind her. What was she doing here? Surely this was folly, stumbling around in the dark looking for a lost oar that may or may not be in the cave, while at any moment Leigh, or worse, the hordes of crabs, could come and find her. What then? She would be trapped.

She gripped her knife for support and stood up. As she put weight onto her right foot, pain lanced her ankle. She grunted and cursed once more, having not initially realised she had hurt herself in that last fall. If ever there was a sign she should turn back, that was it.

As she hobbled forward, careful to remember the location of the previous two obstacles that tripped her, she pondered her next move. The question of the boat was an interesting one. She considered it could still be an option, even without the missing oar, but only if they launched it when the tide was going out. The tide would take them out and away from the island, and then… well she guessed they would be at the mercy of the sea, but at least they would be away from here. And Jorge was returning tomorrow. There was a chance he would find them in transit, though the sea was a big space.

It was a risky plan. Was it any more or less risky than spending another night here? That was something she would have to decide with Marianne. But for now, she should try to drag the boat out of here, injured ankle and all. This might be their only chance at the boat; she could not risk leaving it here and have the hordes of crabs return.

As she hobbled closer to the boat, Inge became aware of a low sound. At first it was barely audible, but it slowly grew in volume the closer she got. It was a familiar sound. One that surrounded them the night before. The sound of clacking claws and shell on stone.

Inge glanced at the darkness about her. She remembered the hordes from the previous night. How they clambered over each other in their masses. She had thought they had all left the cave. She wondered how many stayed behind, hiding under the cloak of darkness about her. She stopped and stared a moment, not certain if she could see movement there or not.

As she waited, the noise grew in volume and intensity. She began to feel uneasy and started to imagine crabs all about her with their claws raised, hidden by the blackness of the cave. She hastened her speed, wondering if she should just forget the boat and get out of here.

Inge's foot hit something hard and she almost fell again as she landed on her sore ankle awkwardly. She stopped. Her intuition told her this was the oar. She could not say why, but she could not shake the feeling this was it. She examined the darkness for movement. Crabs must be all around her. The sound of their clacking echoed off the walls and reverberated through the air. But the oar…

She stepped back and dropped to her knees to feel around for the object. Her hand struck something. It had rough edges, but the top was smooth, like a rock or…

She pulled her hand away just in time to avoid the crab claws that snapped at her. She half fell, and she thrust out her left hand to support her. It landed on a flat hard object. She was about to stand up again and flee when the feeling of the object registered. She reached over with her right hand and felt the object some more, realising quickly that this was the flat of the oar.

She picked it and rose to her feet, elated by her accidental find. Perhaps luck was finally falling her way. Using the oar as a makeshift crutch, she hurried towards the boat. She could barely believe it. The boat was intact and now she had the second oar. All she had to do next was pull the boat out onto the beach and summon Marianne. She could barely believe it. They were going to do it. They were going to escape this infernal island and that psychopath Leigh and his stupid love fantasies. It was going to happen. She could feel it.

As she closed on the boat and cave entrance, it began to grow noticeably lighter around her. She started to make out the movement around her. The walls and corners of the cave were alive with movement. Shiny carapaces glinted dimly in the growing light. A few feet to her left, Inge saw a crab the size of a dinner plate scuttling sideways, pacing her. She dared not look behind, realising there may be many more in pursuit behind her.

Inge broke into a trot. She wanted to push on faster, but it was the best she could do with the pain in her ankle and the oar for a crutch. Sand kicked up behind her as the oar cut divots in the sand, and around her the volume and intensity of the clicking grew the closer she got to the boat. From the corner of her eye, she spotted the crab that had been pacing her had kept up with her increased pace.

She began to breathe hard and the weakness of not having anything to eat this day began to weigh on her. Her legs felt heavy and weak, and for a moment she thought she might stumble, but the thought of the chasing horde running all over her spurred her on.

At last, she reached the boat. She stopped and turned to see if the swarm would overrun her as she tried to pull the boat out. But for the moment they held back, as if waiting for a cue. She threw the oar into the boat, puzzling what their cue might be.

A quick glance at the boat told her there was too much sand inside. All the sand would add extra weight and slow her down. The sand sitting in the boat was dry and loose, and it would take forever to dig out. Her best bet was to raise the boat on its side to tip the excess sand out.

She leaned over and lifted the gunwale of the opposite side of the boat up towards her. It was heavy, and with her right ankle sprained is it was, she pushed hard and carried most of the strain with her left. The sand spilled around her feet and she took a step back. She lifted her right foot to take pressure off her injured ankle. In her momentary distraction, she failed to notice the crab that had been pacing her had crept forwards.

The crab reached out with its claw, pinching the thin skin under Inge's ankle. He shrieked and jumped, landing on her injured right ankle. The ankle twisted, unable to bear the sudden weight, and she fell with the boat toppling down over her. She landed on her stomach with the boat crashing around her, covering her world in darkness.

She winced, her ankle stinging with pain. The distance between the gunwales and the bench seat was small, and as she lay under the boat, she felt the seats press into the small of her back and her thighs. She had very little room to move and, worse, her hair had been loose and was now caught under one of the gunwales.

Inge swore softly, cursing herself over the accident. She dug her hands in the sand and tried pushing herself up, but it was like trying to do a push-up with two people sitting on your back. After a moment she gave up, breathing quickly and taking stock of her situation.

Marianne, or someone, would need to come and lift the boat from on top of her. Until then, she was stuck. Marianne, at least, knew where she was, and when she realised Inge had been gone too long, she would come and investigate. Inge just had to wait. At least she was safe for now. It was uncomfortable and cramped under the boat, but as long as she was in here and the crabs were out there, she was safe.

Inge calmed her breathing while listening for the crabs. She could still hear the distinct clicking of their claws. She wondered if it was a form of communication. Could they be planning and plotting how to get to her with their clicking? She shivered and pushed the thought aside. Leigh had put thoughts into her head with his yammering up at the ruins. Crabs were just dumb animals. She did not want to assign more intelligence to these things than she needed to.

It was cramped and uncomfortable under the boat, but she could deal with it for the time being. But her hair caught under the gunwale bothered her. She clutched the hair next to her head in her fist and pulled it from under the gunwale. There was a short, loud sound, like the scraping of rope against wood. The clicking stopped.

The only sound Inge could now hear was that of her own shallow breathing. The silence of the cave beyond the hull of the boat was oppressive, weighing down on her heavier than the boat itself. She dared not move, fearful that any sound would echo through the cave as loud as a rock concert. The silence may only have lasted seconds, but in the isolation of complete darkness with fear creeping through your soul, it could well have been an eternity. Then the silence was broken as the sound of scratching started.

The sound was faint at first, just tickling the lower limits of her hearing but slowly it grew in volume. At first it only came from around the edges of the boat, where the gunwales met the sand. The sound slowly rose, lifting up around the hull before enveloping it completely. It echoed around the small space that held her, and she imagined the whole surface of the boat hull above her crawling with crabs.

For a long time the sound continued, and the crabs crawling overhead sounded as busy as bees in a hive. But when she listened closely, she identified another sound in this mix. It was drowned by the scratching at first, but quickly the sound was becoming louder and more prominent. It was the sound of splintering wood.

Suddenly there was a loud crack, followed by silence. Then slowly the ticking resumed. Only this time the ticking was different. It was not the same random, multitudinous clicking the crabs usually did. Not this time. This time the crabs were synchronised. They all clacked together, like the clapping of a crowd at a sporting event. The clacking was slow at first, but increased in tempo with each successive click.

Inge began to panic. Nothing about this situation was normal or natural. She squirmed against the boat, again trying in vain to move under its weight. Then she tried pushing it up, but it felt even heavier than before.

She squirmed and pushed against the boat as the clicking in the cave rose in speed and intensity. She worried at what point it would hit a crescendo and what would happen next. She did not have to wait long, as the clicking of claws sped up so fast that the clicks almost blurred together into one continuous sound, when another loud crack sounded above her and light suddenly filtered in. Inge turned her head to see one of the rotted timbers of the hole pulled away, leaving a sizeable hole above her.

The slow clicking began again and the process repeated. She tried squirming free again but only succeeded in chafing her skin against the sand and wooden seat of the boat. This time the loud crack came from near her feet. Despite her rational mind failing to comprehend it, the crabs were pulling the boat apart.

Inge waited for the clicking to start again. But this time there was nothing. Above her head, the eyes of the first curious crab appeared in the opening. She failed to notice it at first, but when her eyes caught the movement, she saw the two long eyestalks bearing those cold, oval eyes looking back down at her. The crab waited a moment longer, then stepped forward and dropped into the boat with Inge. A second pair of eyes appeared at the breach.

Inge scooped a handful of sand and flicked it at the crab. It immediately rose up onto its legs and raised its claws aggressively. The second crab dropped into the boat. Two more sets of eyes appeared in the hole above her.

Inge threw more sand, trying to push the invaders back. But more crabs dropped through the hole. She cursed and swore at them, flinging handfuls of sand and flailing her arms to keep them at bay. But more crabs were dropping into the space by the second, and some of the new arrivals were braver than the first, slowly edging closer to Inge with each moment.

Suddenly pain tore at Inge's feet. She tried to raise her head to look behind her. She made out a shadow falling into the space behind her. Crabs were coming through the rear hole as well.

While she was momentarily distracted, one of the bigger and braver crabs near her head launched forwards, its large claw snapping at her face. She pulled back, avoiding direct contact with her face, but the claw caught her by the nose ring.

The crab pulled, and Inge screamed as she felt the skin of her nose stretch and tear. She grabbed the claw with her two hands and tried to pry the claw open. It was one of the crabs with one large and one small claw. It was the large claw that held her, and she was amazed at the strength of the crab. She wrenched at the claw as the pain in her nose intensified. She felt blood dripping from the wound. The crab retaliated against her by latching onto a finger with its other claw and squeezing.

More pain speared up through her body from her legs. This time behind the knee as she felt another crab latch onto a fold of skin. She tried moving her legs, but she was stuck fast. She felt another crab climb up onto her calves.

Emboldened by the first crab's success on Inge's nose, other crabs closed in around her. Inge felt tugging and tearing on her hair. She tried to shift her head up, when one crab clambered up and latched onto her ear. Inge screamed. She released one hand from the claw on her nose to grab at her ear when the nose crab succeeded in wrenching her nose ring out. She screamed in pain as the scent of blood overwhelmed her senses.

Crabs continued falling through the hole, crowding the cramped space under the boat where Inge lay trapped and at their mercy. As the mob grew, so did their boldness. Soon they were all over her, pinching and tearing at her skin. In her hair, on her face, over her neck and shoulders, inside her shirt, on her back, on her buttocks, legs and feet. There were too many around her and no way to keep them at bay. She felt the pain of hundreds of wounds at once as they clawed and clung, nipped and pulled and ripped and tore at her flesh. Blood seeped from her wounds and the cramped space inside the boat was thick with the iron scent of her blood.

Inge tried keeping the crabs from her face, but now at least a dozen crabs clung to her hands and pulled at her fingers. She could do little to keep them away, and those that clung on were unperturbed by her thrashing about. A claw reached out and ripped off some skin just above her eye. Inge blinked, but her vision only blurred with blood as she realised one eyelid had just been torn away.

She screamed and screamed. She called for Marianne, for Dirk and for Andy. Hell, she even called for Leigh. Facing him may not have been the lesser of two fates after all.

But no help came. More crabs dropped into the space around her, clawing and ripping with ravenous hunger. Where her skin was punctured, claws forced their way in, snipping and pulling at the flesh around the open wound.

For Inge, there was no chance of rescue. Even if someone had heard the screams, hordes of crabs that scoured the surface of the boat would have kept them at bay. There was no chance they would let this meal get away from them.

Inge was suffering a mercilessly slow and painful death as she was painstakingly pulled apart by the crabs and eaten alive. She screamed and screamed until her throat was raw with pain, and then she screamed more. She was still alive as the crabs peeled back the skin from her body and began feasting on the muscles underneath. She felt them pull at her tendons and cut through her body with their sharp claws. When she gave up on rescue ever arriving, she ached for them to kill her and end the pain. But there was no easy death to be had and the agony continued on relentlessly.

If anyone had stood at the cave entrance and timed the ritual, they would have counted three hours of straight screaming as Inge was consumed alive by the crabs. At dusk they began to disperse, leaving Inge alive and in pain but trapped under the boat, too weak to escape. Her meat was secure, and would continue to provide further meals for them in the days ahead. But more meat was needed, and as dusk closed on the island, they knew they had to secure more food for the time ahead. For they had learned the pattern of the man in the boat, and knew that he would take away what they did not eat not long after the sun rose again.

Inge continued to whimper long after the sun had set. She lay in complete darkness and silence. The only senses with something left to communicate to her mind screamed only agony and blood. Her body was ruined and her brain too scrambled to fully comprehend all the damage and pain that scoured the wreck of her being. Hours passed and Inge endured nothing but agony and torment from every part of her torn body. It was well past midnight when she finally, and mercifully, passed out. If she was lucky, she would not wake again.

27

Tears clouded Marianne's eyes as she tied the final knot on the makeshift bandage around Dirk's injured leg. When she was convinced it was tight enough, she placed two fingers against Dirk's neck and felt the weak throbbing of his pulse. A small crushed crab, no bigger than a euro coin, lay by her knee. Content her job was done, she allowed her head to drop and she let the sobs that had been clawing at her insides finally go free.

It had been far more traumatic than she could have ever imagined. Dirk had bucked and kicked like crazy as she fished through his wound for the rogue crab. It had been just as wily as the previous one, crawling between folds of meat to stay out of reach. The very touch of Dirk's warm, wet flesh alone made her dry retch, and to feel around for a moving target in there while Dirk writhed in pain had almost broken her.

Wiping the tears, Marianne looked around the mess she had made in the tent. It looked, and smelled, like an abattoir. Bloodied water lay in puddles around her from when she had flushed the wound. The tent stank of blood and the air was suffocating and humid. She unzipped the tent and gulped at the fresh air. She needed to clean up the awful mess she had made inside.

She eyed the ruins carefully as she exited the tent. There were no clawed little monsters about, but she remembered how quickly they had materialised in the ruins previously and knew she needed to keep her eyes sharp.

Her first priority was to mop up the mess in the tent. She could not leave Dirk lying in his own blood like that. The group's packs lay together near where she set the tent. Her first instinct was to dive into her own pack and pick some of her older clothes to clean up with. But as she knelt down, she stopped.

Marianne tilted her head slightly and looked at Leigh's pack. Her face curled up into a snarl as she looked over his colourful pack proudly emblazoned with the Australian flag. She leaned forward and opened the pack. Call it revenge for throwing a rock at her, or for acting weird about her friend Inge, or for pushing his mate Andy over the edge of a cliff, or just for being a dickhead in general, but Marianne decided it should be Leigh's clothes that should be stained and ruined by the blood, not hers. She could not think of a better way of saying 'fuck you' to the psycho in that moment.

After picking a few t-shirts from the pack, Marianne looked down toward the field. The sun was getting low on the horizon and Inge still had not returned. Before returning to the tent, Marianne quickly checked over the cliff. The white sand was mostly shrouded in shadow, but it was still clear to see there was no sign of Inge.

Marianne re-entered the tent and zipped the door closed behind her. She lay the t-shirts out on the floor and began soaking up the bloody pink water. As she cleaned, she heard scuffing footsteps outside the tent. Her heart leapt. She picked up the sopping wet t-shirts and opened the tent. She crawled out, carrying the dripping shirts with her.

"Jesus Inge, what took you so…"

Her words dropped away as she realised it was not Inge before her, but Leigh. He turned and stared at her with blank, empty eyes. A shiver ran down her spine.

"Where's Inge?" she asked, switching to English.

"I don't know," replied Leigh in a cold, monotonous voice.

Marianne bit her bottom lip and turned and strode to the cliff and peered over. She looked down towards the cave and then along the beach but as before, there was no sign of Inge. Marianne sucked in a deep breath through her nostrils and swallowed hard. She stood and turned to face Leigh.

"What have you done to her?"

"Who?"

"Inge." Marianne could hear the cracks in her voice. She hoped she was coming across stronger than she felt.

Leigh stared a moment. "I've done nothing."

Then Leigh turned, spying his opened pack on the ground. He turned back to Marianne and pointed to the dripping t-shirts she held. "Are those my clothes?"

Marianne's heart skipped a beat. "Y-Yes."

Leigh's face darkened and his mouth twitched. "You couldn't use the dead man's clothes?"

"There's no dead man here."

He stared at her blankly for a moment. "Andy's still alive?"

"Yes. But he can't feel his body from the waist down. He could be paralysed for life."

"That's a shame."

Marianne did not like the coldness of his voice. "Which part is the shame? That he survived or that he's paralysed?"

But if she expected Leigh to answer, none was forthcoming. He turned back to his pack and started sorting through his clothes. Marianne felt her lip quiver as she turned and once more looked down the beach for a sign of Inge. There was movement far below. What appeared as small grey flecks were emerging from the water and out of the cave below her. Those flecks could be only one thing: crabs. Marianne pulled away from the edge and half-stumbled, half-walked across the ruins to get a better view down the empty hillside.

"God, Inge," she whispered to the wind, "where are you?"

With shaking hands, Marianne squeezed the bloody water out of the t-shirts. Her longing eyes scanned the landscape below, pleading for any sign of Inge. Marianne clenched her eyes shut, silently wishing Inge would appear and arrest the fears that were invading her mind. She opened them once more. The sight of the empty landscape below quickly blurred and Marianne wiped a tear from her cheek.

Behind her, Leigh had started assembling the small sticks and wood into a pile. Marianne made a snap decision, turning and hurrying past Leigh to duck into the tent. She hoped it was not obvious that she was hurrying. She zipped the door tight behind her, before dropping her head into her hands.

Something had happened to Inge. She knew it. And that bastard Leigh was behind it.

Marianne lifted her head to look at Dirk. He looked like death incarnate. His skin was so pale and his breathing so shallow, even if he did wake, he would be in no position to do anything other than continue to lay there and rest.

With Dirk incapacitated, Andy pushed off a cliff and probably paralysed, and Inge missing, Marianne had to face the night ahead with hordes of creepy, marauding crabs and a potentially psychopathic killer.

Her bottom lip quivered and she bit down on it. All her life, other people had fought her battles. If it was not her parents, it was her friends. And if it was not her friends, it was Dirk. Someone always stood in the breach to protect her. But now, as she needed protection like never before, she found herself utterly alone against unimaginable enemies.

She sucked in a deep breath through her nose. So be it, she decided. Just because people always fought in her place, it did not mean she was a shrinking violet. Marianne could be tough. She just had not needed to call on those reserves before. But she was strong, and tonight she would prove it.

Marianne wiped the tears from her eyes with the back of her hand, vowing she would cry no more this night. She took three more deep breaths of resolve.

She needed Leigh. She could not face the night invasion of the crabs alone. But if it came to it, she would fight Leigh. She was prepared for that.

Nodding to herself and quietly whispering self-affirmations, Marianne set about finishing the clean-up of the tent. She allowed a small smile as she did so, glad she had chosen Leigh's clothing for the job. That would show him she had spine. That she was not afraid of him.

Little did Marianne know it would be the last smile that would ever cross her lips.

28

Andy's eyes flickered open as consciousness swam back to him once more. For a moment he thought the fight and subsequent fall may have all been a bad dream, but as he looked up at the cliff-face ahead of him, the nightmare came back to reality.

He propped himself up on one elbow and took stock of himself. His skin he could still feel radiated heat and looked an angry red colour. Great, he thought, now I can add sunburn and risk of skin cancer to my woes. His stomach ached with hunger and his mouth was dry, so he reached for the bottle of water Marianne had thrown down and took a swig. It was already getting low, hopefully she would check in soon and pass another bottle down.

The sun was low in the sky now and it would be getting dark soon. He must have been out a few hours.

Within minutes of waking, Andy became bored. He hated to think of himself as a tech addict, but he knew deep down he was. He could not escape it, he had grown up with technology and since devoting himself to being an influencer, technology had been like a drug. Whenever he posted anything new online, he became as jumpy as a cat. He needed to check his phone every five seconds for likes or comments. He could not help it. It was just how he was. An addict. When Leigh had started observing this behaviour, he started counting how many times Andy checked his phone within the first hour of making a post. Andy's record was two hundred and fifty times. Or so Leigh had claimed.

And contact with the world was what he needed now. Not, as you might expect, to call for help. No, what he longed for more than anything else was to see how many likes and comments that last picture he posted, the one of them all in the boat on the pier before they left, had garnered.

And what of the video and photos Marianne had made for him? He did not even know if those were any good. His followers expected, and deserved, a high quality of imagery from him. This incident was going to be a significant post. It was life defining. The last thing he needed was a blurred photo or a shaky video to ruin it. He wished he could review what she had done.

He sighed and shook his head.

"Ugh, I am such a fucking addict," he murmured to himself, "and a pathetic one at that. I should be worried about how I'm going to get out of here but instead I'm thinking about likes and comments."

"Hey," a voice called from above. It was Marianne.

"Hey," he called back.

"You're awake. How are you?"

He huffed. "As good as can be expected I suppose." He waited, expecting she had more to say, but she just watched on. It was starting to feel awkward, when he remembered their earlier conversation. "How about the boat? Is it any good?"

Marianne stared a second, then looked behind her for a moment before turning back to him. "Inge hasn't returned."

Andy glanced over towards the setting sun. She would want to be getting back soon. He looked back up to Marianne, and noticed she was wiping a tear away.

"What about Leigh? Where is he?"

"He's here."

Andy felt suddenly ill. He reached out for his bottle and took a few short sips of water. After taking a couple of deep breaths, he looked back up at Marianne. "Can he hear me right now?"

Marianne looked behind her once more, staring for a few seconds before turning back to Andy. "Only me."

Andy nodded slightly and swallowed. "You probably have over a hundred questions you want to ask me right now but you can't because he will hear you. You probably want to know if Leigh is capable of doing something bad to Inge. The thing is, I can't say for sure. I mean, I never saw him hurt anyone. But there were rumours…" Andy's voice trailed off. He took another sip of water to compose himself before continuing. "In our last year of high school, he was really keen on this girl, Angela. He used to walk her home after school. He liked her a lot, and I know he was going to confess his love to her. Anyway, one day she just stopped coming to school. Just like that. And suddenly everything got weird. Leigh's parents had lawyers. The school had lawyers. And Leigh was not telling me shit. I don't know what happened to Angela, she never came back to the school and Leigh never spoke of her, but another guy I know reckons he saw her at a shopping mall one time with her arm in a cast and bruising on her face."

Andy paused. Marianne was wiping more tears from her face.

"I'm sorry, I should have told you this before, but I still have this mindset of protecting him because he's my best mate. I've been friends with Leigh for as long as I can remember," Andy paused and looked about himself. "Sometimes you overlook and forgive people for their flaws just to stay friends with them. It's cost me a lot over time. Especially now."

Andy took another sip. He knew he was rambling, but he suddenly felt he needed to come clean about the past and tell it all. He owed Marianne that.

"I guess what I am trying to say here is it is possible he did something to Inge. He's not normal with girls. He never has been. If Inge doesn't come back… well… just be careful ok? Don't mention her or do anything to upset him. Just bite your tongue and get through the night so we can all get the fuck off this island. Just look after yourself and don't give him any reason to get upset with you. And if Inge doesn't come back, we deal with it when we are safe back in Bocas Town. Understand? We deal with the shit back in Bocas Town. You and me together."

Marianne listened intently, wiping tears from her face as he spoke. After absorbing his words for a moment, she finally spoke. "Okay."

For a moment they were awkwardly silent. Andy started wondering if it was a mistake telling Marianne about Angela. He'd probably just freaked her out. Now she would spend the night paranoid, which may only make the situation worse. He needed her to get through the night. She could be his only hope of rescue from here. He had to steady her.

"Hey Marianne," he called. "Listen, about Angela…"

But she stopped him with a gesture from her hand and turned away from the edge to look behind her. She said something then, but he could not make it out. Finally, she turned and looked back down at Andy.

"Hey, sorry to do this, but I have to go. The crabs are on their way." She stopped and bit her lip, looking down at him sadly. "Do you think you'll be okay down there on your own?"

He gave her a smile that he hoped did not look as hollow as it felt. "Of course. I mean, it's not like I have any alternative here. I'll be fine. Just drop me a couple of water bottles and look after yourself. You're the one on the frontline, after all."

Marianne nodded slowly as her eyes scanned the craggy rocks of the cliff faces about him. "I suppose you're right. It's not as though those crabs can climb the cliffs or anything." Without further ado, she pulled away from view.

The smile on Andy's face died the moment she disappeared, her words having brought back the memory of the curious crab from earlier that day. It had crawled over the edge in a spider like manner. He twisted his body as best he could to view the spot he last saw it. Where had that little bastard gone?

29

Having dropped two more bottles down to Andy, Marianne turned away from the cliff edge and returned to where Leigh had begun stoking up the fire. The sky was darkening quickly, as it had done the night previous, and below them as she looked down the hill, she could see the ground was already alive with movement. She shivered, and crossed her arms around herself, though the shiver had little to do with her being cold.

"So, how is he?" Leigh asked without looking up.

"He's okay, all things considered."

Leigh stood up and faced her. He stood a full foot taller than her, and as he stood now, he positioned his body close so he could tower above her. He stared hard into her eyes. His eyes were lit by the flickering light of the fire, but Marianne could see only coldness inside. Marianne resisted the urge to break eye contact or step back. She could not let him intimidate her.

"It wasn't on purpose, you understand? I didn't know the cliff was there. The whole thing. The fight, the push, Andy falling. It was all an accident. You got it?"

Marianne realised her hands were shaking and put them behind her back. "If you say so."

"I do say so."

That seemed to be the end of what Leigh had to say, yet he remained standing over her. She looked up, willing herself not to pull away or break eye contact. Don't let him win, she told herself, don't get intimidated. But he remained standing over her, and it was quickly becoming too much for her to handle.

"Are we done here?" she asked with as much gusto as she could muster.

"I just want to make sure we have our stories straight, that's all," Leigh said with an aching slowness.

Around her, the ticking sound that haunted her the previous night was slowly becoming more and more audible. The tide of crabs was coming, and in that moment, Marianne was unsure what she feared more: the crabs or Leigh. As she stared into those cold, dead eyes she wondered what he had done to that girl Angela, what he had done to Inge, and what he could do to her. For the crabs, it was primal hunger that drove them. They came to feed. But Leigh was another matter. He was a dark soul with a damaged mind. The crabs, the hellish nightmare that they were, were just following their instincts. She could forgive them that. But Leigh was supposed to be a rational, thinking person. What he did was unforgivable. If it came to a choice, she would choose crabs every time.

"Yes, we have our stories straight," she said as she tried to keep her voice steady. "You didn't know the cliff was there. Andy's fall was an accident."

Despite agreeing to his terms, Leigh continued to stare down at her. The clicking became louder, and Marianne ached to look away. Movement flicked at the edges of her vision, and she was sure that already the crabs were breaching the boundaries of the ruin. But she held strong, refusing to be intimidated.

"Good," he said at last, before turning away.

No longer held by his gaze, Marianne stepped away to check the zip on the tent where Dirk lay. She knew it was zipped tight, but she needed to walk away to catch her breath and regain her composure. Her legs were like jelly, and the simple act of moving a few feet to the tent felt like walking over a trampoline while other people jumped around her.

Marianne took in deep breaths as her shaking hands unnecessarily checked the zip. She held onto the last breath a moment longer, and as she was breathing out, she noticed the first crab entering the ruin. It stopped as she spotted it, as if sensing it had been caught. The sun had almost disappeared now, and the firelight cast a sinister dancing shadow behind the little monster.

Just then, a second crab emerged from the shadows behind the first one. Then more movement caught Marianne's eye to her right. As she looked about, Marianne realised other crabs had breached the ruins too. With rising panic, she realised tonight would not be like the last one. Tonight, they would not be held at bay by barriers of bags or stone. They were coming in uninvited.

"Hey, you going to check that zip all night?"

"What?" Marianne asked, still half in her reverie.

"I need you over here to help me keep the crabs out of the ruin."

"It's too late for that."

"What?"

"They are already in here, Leigh."

He turned and as he spotted their malevolent forms in the dancing firelight, his eyes widened with fear. More crabs entered the ruins as he watched. They climbed over rocks and crawled sideways across the ruin. One found a gap between two stones and, having pushed itself through, raised its claws above its head and clicked them together. More crabs began to appear in the hole and started crawling through.

"They're communicating by clicking," Leigh said breathlessly.

But as Leigh stared in wonderment and understanding, Marianne began growing impatient and fearful. With just the two of them alone, they were not set up to defend against marauders on all sides. But Leigh was spellbound, and Marianne realised she needed to take control if she was to survive the night.

"We need to make a tight circle, like we had last night," she said. She dashed to the side and grabbed her backpack to drag it over by the fire. She turned to see Leigh standing and watching. She wanted to slap him. "Help me, before they overrun the ruins completely."

Leigh blinked and the light came on in his mind. He joined in and soon they had the bags and tents packed into a tight circle under Marianne's instruction. It was very similar to the previous night's setup, but much smaller so all sides were within reach at all times, with the fire forming a barrier on one side and the tent on the other. It would enable them to stand back-to-back to ward off any crabs trying to enter. Assuming, of course, they did not try entering all at once. Then they would have a problem.

It struck her how odd it might have looked for anyone who might look in at this moment. Two people, strangers until but a few days ago, who were mortal enemies as far as Marianne was concerned, standing back-to-back brandishing torches and sticks as an army of crabs circled them. Was there any more absurd scene anywhere on this planet in this moment? She wondered.

The crabs continued to mill around the ruins as the last rays of light dipped below the distant horizon. The clicking sound grew in intensity and volume as the light died, and as the darkness shrouded the island the clicking hit fever pitch. Marianne wanted to place her hands over her ears to block the nightmare sound out. The moon shone down, lighting the glinting wet bodies of the crabs around them. With the onset of darkness, their numbers seemed to increase threefold in seconds. They clustered around in what must have been thousands. Marianne could not spot a single square of ground not covered by a crab.

Unconsciously, Marianne took half a step backwards. Her back came into contact with Leigh's. Instinctively, she wanted to cringe away from his touch, yet knowing he was there provided a level of comfort. It was a confusing moment as she weighed repulsion against security that someone had her back.

The touch was only momentary, however, as Leigh leaned forward to knock a curious crab who had climbed up onto one of the packs. Marianne felt momentary terror when she saw the first of the skeletal crab legs squirm into view. She slammed her wood down, only to see another pair of oval eyes on raised stalks appear close by. She swung clumsily and missed, but the eyes ducked away.

The first crab reappeared in the same spot and she whacked down again. Suddenly, she felt like she was playing an absurd, dark game of Whack-a-Mole. She remembered playing it as a child. But the delight she felt as a giggling eight-year-old whacking each mole in the head as it popped up was far removed from the desperate situation she now faced. The moles were fun and harmless. The crabs were creepy and would pinch and overwhelm if she let them under her guard.

But that is how it played out. Marianne and Leigh, back-to-back, whacking crabs as they crept into view. For a time, Marianne settled into a rhythm, thrusting and hitting effectively to keep them at bay. But as the night wore on, she realised this was less her playing Whack-a -Crab, and more the crabs playing her. She was already weak from a day without food and filled with emotional stress. Now the constant movement was like an aerobic workout she did not need and it was draining her quicker than a crack in a water tank. As she aimed another clumsy hit, she realised that she had not hit one cleanly yet.

"This isn't achieving anything," she complained as another crab appeared.

"What do you mean?"

"All I am succeeding in doing right now is getting myself exhausted. I feel like we're being played."

Leigh was quiet a moment, though she sensed him moving behind her.

"Me too," he said at last, "I don't think I've killed one yet. So, what should we do?"

Again, he was deferring to her leadership. Only this time Marianne had no answer. If they stopped, the crabs would breach their precious sanctuary and be all over them. They could flee into the tent, hiding behind the canvas barrier and hope for the best. It's a plan she had considered, but what if they really could break through the thin fabric of the tent? Last night they hadn't, but last night was not a concerted effort either. If they really tried, she did not want to know if they could or not, because if they could then no tent would be safe and Dirk could never be saved. As long as she and Leigh stayed out here, the less their attention would be on the tent that held the defenceless body of Dirk.

"I don't know," she conceded. "But I'm open to ideas."

But if Leigh had any ideas, none was forthcoming. The game of Whack-a-Crab went on.

As time passed, Marianne felt her body slowing. Her shoulder began to ache, and her hand felt sore from the ungainly shape of the wood. Her legs were heavy, and each passing swing was clumsier than the last. Exhaustion was setting in, and the night still had many hours to run.

When her right hand began cramping from the awkward hold she had on the wood, she swapped hands over and continued to strike. But as she struck down on one crab, the wood slipped from her grip with the impact, clattering over the opposite side and into the hordes. Almost immediately, crabs poured over the breaches unfettered by her defences.

Before she had even reached for a replacement, the small patch of ground they held was invaded. Crabs crawled between their legs, snapping their claws aggressively.

"What the hell?" Leigh cursed as he found himself suddenly attacked from under his feet.

Marianne started stamping her feet, crushing the little monsters that dared come near. She retrieved a flaming piece of wood from the fire, swinging recklessly about her. Leigh, too, stamped his feet and crushed crabs underfoot, leaving their small area littered with broken shell and sticky crab innards.

"This is fucked," Leigh said, "they won't stop until they have killed us."

"We have nothing to give them. They ate everything we had last night."

"We have Dirk."

Marianne's blood ran cold. To think it, was evil in itself. But to say it out loud to her so casually, so easily, was beyond anything she could bear.

"Are you fucking kidding me? How dare you! How can you suggest such a thing?"

"We have to start thinking of saving ourselves, Marianne. We won't make it through the night if they don't feed."

"You'd be killing him."

"He's as good as dead already. You saw him, Marianne. He won't make it. Deep down you know it's true. You need to accept that, because we can use him to save us."

She shook her head. "No, I won't do it."

Tears blurred her eyes as she swung her stick at the crabs. So much for the promise she had made to herself not to cry. The crabs were coming in larger numbers, sensing their moment. Soon the crabs were about their feet, snapping at their exposed legs and rending cuts in their skin. Leigh swore and started swinging wildly, stamping and shouting like a crazy man. The insane roar that issued from his throat caused Marianne to shiver.

Crabs continued to pour over the bags in torrents around them. The numbers were too great to hold off, and Marianne ceased trying to keep them at bay but instead focused on keeping them from clawing and climbing her legs. The noise around her was growing as the crabs clicked their claws in frenzied excitement.

The sound of a zipper suddenly brought her attention sharp and she looked up to see Leigh opening the tent.

"What are you doing?" she screamed above the clacking din.

Leigh did not answer, but instead stepped inside the tent, shaking off crabs that clung to him. Marianne did not hesitate and followed him through, afraid he might zip it closed and hold it shut behind him.

Leigh crushed a stray crab that entered by clinging to her shoe and straightened to stand over her and look her in the eye. Thankfully, he could not straighten as the low roof of the tent forced him to crouch, and for the first time their eyes were level as they stood face to face. Around them the crabs scratched at the tent canvas.

"This is impossible," Leigh said. "There are too many. We have to give them food so they leave us alone."

Marianne stood defiantly. "Don't you dare touch Dirk. You hear me? You leave Dirk alone."

He stared her in the eyes a moment longer, daring her to look away, but she held strong. Frustrated, he turned, breathing heavily and cracking his knuckles. He moved about the small space with a restless energy. The crabs scratched at the sides of the tent, their shadowed claws looming large on the canvas. Leigh approached one wall and kick it hard enough that the whole tent wobbled with the impact.

"Go away you little fucks," he roared, "leave me alone."

Marianne set the torch down in the centre of the tent and eased herself down beside Dirk. She drew her knees up to her chest and hugged them while she watched Leigh warily. She was glad for the moment to sit, but her senses told her she could not afford to relax.

Leigh continued to kick at the walls of the tent while hurling expletive ridden insults at the crabs. Eventually he tired and sank to his knees and dropped his head into his palms. The clicking and scratching was all around them, playing like a nightmare dirge of some macabre orchestra. Quiet sobs escaped Leigh's mouth.

"It wasn't supposed to go like this," he said between sobs.

Of course not, Marianne thought. But what could they reasonably have expected coming to an island as shrouded in mystery as this? No wonder it had been kept off the maps and out of the tourist books. This island was a death trap.

"We could never have known the island would be like this," Marianne responded in an attempt to settle him down.

"It's not that," Leigh continued, "I'm talking about Inge. She was supposed to be with me."

Marianne drew a shaking breath in. Oh God, she thought, he's lost it.

Leigh turned his head to regard her. His cheeks were streaking with tears and his eyes red. "You're a girl. Help me understand. What is wrong with me? Why doesn't any girl want my love?"

"Look, Leigh, I don't think now is the time…"

"Aarrgggh shut up. We're going to die here on this shit fucking island so you might as well tell me. What's the big secret I don't know? What am I missing? Why don't the girls I like want me?"

Marianne could see he was clenching his fists so tight now his knuckles were as white as bleached paper.

"It's all just so unfair."

He was shouting through clenched teeth now. Marianne regarded him like she would a wounded dog. He was hurting, but it did not mean he was not dangerous.

"Not all girls are alike, Leigh. I'm sure there is someone out there who would really love your attention…"

Leigh scoffed. "That's what people keep telling me. But every girl I love only likes me as a friend." Leigh wiped his cheeks with his palms, them fixed his gaze once more on her. "What about you?"

"What about me?"

"Would you go out with me?"

"I already have a boyfriend."

Leigh rolled his eyes in frustration. "Pretend Dirk is dead. We've just met. Would you go out with me?"

Marianne swallowed. "But Dirk's not dead."

"Pretend he is." Leigh's voice was rising.

"No, I'm not playing that game. I don't want to think about Dirk being dead and you can't make me. I need Dirk alive, because it's all I have to keep me going on."

"Ugh," Leigh grunted, slapping the wall of the tent closest to him in frustration. "You're just like every other slut out there. You all pretend to be nice but inside you are all bitches who like to play games."

He went silent and Marianne decided it best to not talk any further. Marianne hated being in this confined space with him, but she could not go outside. Not anymore. She felt bitterly tired and weak. Her legs were scratched and scabbing with dried blood. Her stomach ached for food. She would do anything to eat and relax in this moment, but Leigh had lost the plot. She needed to stay awake and keep her wits about her.

At last Leigh turned to her again. "He's probably already dead, you know. You haven't checked his pulse in hours."

Marianne's eyes flicked to Dirk's still form and she licked her lips tentatively. It was true. She had not checked Dirk's pulse for a long time now. She had not done it because she was afraid. Dirk was a deathly white. He had lost a lot of blood in both crab extractions. She was afraid checking would only bring forward the news she was dreading. She was afraid for the worst.

"Do it," Leigh sneered, sensing her hesitation. "Do it now. And if he's dead, you have to answer my question."

Marianne turned her head, unwrapped her body and moved slowly towards Dirk's head. As she looked down, she could see no life in him. If he breathed, his breaths were so shallow they made the movement in his chest undetectable. His skin was so white and delicate it could be made from chinaware. His eyes were closed and he lay completely motionless.

Marianne placed her fingers against his neck as a single tear dropped from her eye. She waited a moment.

"He's alive," she announced.

"Then why are you crying?"

"From relief," she answered without hesitation. She kissed Dirk on the forehead and resumed her sitting position. Leigh glared at her suspiciously.

"You know," Leigh said slowly, "it doesn't really matter if he's alive now. He's going to die eventually."

"He just needs to get through the night and the boat trip back to Bocas Town."

Leigh barked a hollow, callous laugh. With his head tilted back, his face was covered by shadow, giving him an evil countenance. "Do you really think Jorge will come back to get us?" Leigh laughed again, causing Marianne to scowl. "Didn't you see the way that little wog sped off after dropping us at the island? He didn't even say goodbye. You know why? He knows, Marianne. He fucking knows. And let me tell you, if I knew about these crabs, I wouldn't be coming back here either."

Marianne clutched herself tighter. The manner in which Jorge had dropped them off was brusque, but that did not mean he was not coming back. Leigh was trying to get under her skin and into her mind. Trying to make her give up hope. She shook her head.

"He's coming back. I'm sure of it."

Leigh gave her a derisive snort. She looked away and watched the shadows of the crabs as they clung and clawed at the tent. In many places, she saw the crabs pinching at the fabric. It held firm, for now. She sensed Leigh's eyes on her, ogling her, but refused to look and acknowledge him. After a few minutes, the moment passed and he looked away again.

Minutes felt like hours as the crabs massed about the outside of the tent, clicking and scraping against the fabric, their shadows looming ominously around the sides with their claws opening and closing like a crude shadow puppet show. Whilst it made Marianne uncomfortable, she remained comforted in the fact that as long as they were still clicking and scraping it meant that they were on the outside and she was safe. Well, safe from them at least.

Leigh was another matter altogether. With every passing moment, she became more and more worried about his behaviour. From the sobbing into his hands, to frustrated curses, to quiet mumbling, to looking at the tent walls wide eyed with fear, his mood seemed to change from minute to minute. He stood up, paced the length of the tent crouched over awkwardly (the distance from one end to the tent to the other being a mere three steps), kicking the sides and shouting obscenities before sitting down again restlessly. Every now and then he would pull an object from his pocket, examine it, and then jam it again into his pocket. He did this three times before Marianne caught a glimpse of the object. It was a small keyring with clogs on it.

Suddenly, there was a great tearing sound. Leigh leapt to his feet.

"They're getting in," he shouted.

Marianne looked about, panic stricken, for the breach in the tent. She reached for the torch, but Leigh snatched it up before she could grab it.

"We need to give them Dirk," Leigh cried. "They need food, we need to think about saving ourselves. It's the only way."

She climbed to her feet, intending to block his path but he brushed her aside effortlessly, sending her tumbling to the floor. Before she could do anymore, Leigh placed his fingers against Dirk's throat. He waited a second before he turned to face Marianne. The torch lit his face from underneath, giving his face the look of a hellish ghost mask.

"He's dead," Leigh announced.

"No," Marianne cried.

Leigh's face turned into a snarl. "He was dead before, wasn't he? You fucking lied to me. You risked my fucking life. We could have thrown his body to the crabs before but you fucking lied."

Leigh stood and tucked the torch under one arm. He dug his hands into Dirk's armpits and began to lift his body.

Marianne pulled herself to her feet. "No," she cried, lurching forward to pull Leigh's arms away. "Leave him alone."

He tried to brush her aside dismissively once more, dropping the torch in the process. Marianne was pushed back, but she retained her footing. She lurched forward and slapped Leigh on the face.

Leigh bellowed in anger. He dropped Dirk, closed his first and swung. The punch connected her with a glancing blow to the side of her head. Her legs immediately collapsed beneath her and she dropped like a stone.

But he was not done there. Marianne gurgled something as she struggled to lift herself up. He hit her again. She went down and stayed down this time. He crouched over her and watched as her eyes rolled in her skull. She was not stopping him from doing this. He had to give them Dirk to save himself.

He hit her two more times for good measure.

30

It had been a dark and lonely night for Andy. He could not have felt more cut off and distant from the rest of the world as he lay paralysed on his little shelf on the side of the cliff. The rock wall cut off any sound of the events above, and all that was audible to him was the whistling of the wind as it passed across the crags and holes of the cliff face and the occasional clicking of bone on stone.

It was the second sound that kept him awake so late. He remembered his visitor from earlier and how nimbly it had climbed along the rocky cliff face. Could all the crabs do that, or was it just that one that had become accustomed to living up here? He could only wonder.

But as the night deepened, he was certain the clicking sound he heard had to be from more than one crab. It had started slowly at first, but as the minutes turned into hours, the frequency increased.

The moon was high in the sky and bright this night. It lit up Andy's little corner of the world clearly enough, and Andy could see he was quite alone on his ledge.

At one point during the day, he had wet his pants. It did not bother him, he could not feel it, but the smell of urine did bother him. Like an unwelcome guest, it stayed about him, hovering in the air to remind him how depressing his current state was. He looked up at the stars and wondered privately how life could get any worse than this.

As the time passed slowly, Andy found himself reflecting on his life to come once he got out of here (because if he did not think about the future, he would be stuck with the depressing present, and he had no idea how they would rescue him off this ledge). He would still be an influencer, that he had already determined, but if he was paralysed, as he believed he was, he needed to find a new audience and new sponsors. He needed to find new and interesting stories.

Could he still take adventure holidays? A lot of the world would now be inaccessible to him. Perhaps he could be a beacon for accessibility awareness, helping not just himself but others who faced the same plight.

But the more he thought about it, the more he became depressed. His only consolation being that he had lived his life to its fullest up to this point. He really did have a life to envy. It's the reason people followed him. To see the parties. The girls. The hinted at debauchery. The travel and adventures. He had done it and left no regrets behind.

Well, maybe not. Maybe one regret. Maybe choosing Leigh over Carly had been the wrong decision. And not for the events that occurred on this island. He regretted it long before coming here. The regret had hit him that time, two months after Andy had told Carly it was not going to work, when he had seen her with another guy. He had always hoped that after healing his friendship with Leigh he could rekindle the flame between them (with Leigh's permission, of course). It had galled him to see she had hooked up with someone else, but unlike Leigh, he let it go and moved on.

The moon was passing overhead now and Andy realised it would soon pass behind the cliff and his ledge would become swallowed by shadow. He listened intently, but the sound of clicking had stopped and his only companion was the wind whistling through the rocks.

He drowsily watched as the moon slowly drifted behind the cliff. The shadow slowly drew across his body like a blanket. But there was no warmth in this blanket, only cold, unforgiving darkness. Andy watched as the shadow swallowed his legs, the blackness of its essence so impenetrable he could see nothing of his body within its folds.

He watched as the shadow crept up to his waist. It seemed almost apt. Now he could not only not feel anything below his waist, he could no longer see it either. It was surreal, as if the bottom half of his body no longer existed.

Andy lay back and closed his eyes. He was feeling sleepy and the night was passing with a painful slowness. He wondered if Inge had returned, and how she and Marianne were coping up there alone with Leigh. He only hoped they could keep their cool. Leigh was manageable, so long as you played him right. Take charge and do not give him reason to do anything but follow you.

It was on these thoughts Andy's mind dwelled as he drifted off to sleep. The crabs, who waited patiently in the cracks and shadows, noted the change in breathing pattern, and slowly emerged from their dark corners to investigate.

31

Marianne woke to a world of pain. Her head ached far worse than any hangover she had been forced to endure, and the whole left side of her face burned as though it was cooking in a pan on the fire. Her mouth was dry and tasted of blood.

She lay on her back inside the tent. It was light now. The sun was up. There were no sounds of clicking or scratching on the tent either. The crabs had gone. She glanced about the tent. Dirk was gone too. As was Leigh. At least she could be thankful of that.

As tears bubbled in her eyes, she noticed there was something odd about her vision. She lifted a hand in front of her face and waved it from side to side. She had no vision out of her left eye.

She placed her hand to her face and felt the sensitive, swollen skin. It was crusted with blood and stung at her light touch. The bloating was worst around her eye, where it had closed over completely. Marianne thought she may have a broken eye socket.

Too pained to sit, she felt around her body. She was still clothed and the only places she felt pain was her head and neck. She breathed a sigh of relief. At least Leigh had not raped her after the attack.

She lay a while longer to rest and prepare herself for the agonizing pain of sitting up. Outside she heard someone whistling. It was a jaunty, playful tune. It made her feel sick.

A water bottle lay discarded on the floor of the tent not far to her right. Dryness scratched at her throat and she forced herself up to a sitting position. The world spun, and she had to steady herself while she waited for the ground to level out again. Finally, it did, and as she reached out for the bottle, the tent zip opened behind her.

Leigh entered the tent and scooped up the bottle she was reaching for before she could clutch it. He stood over her for a minute before stepping around her to crouch in front of her. He studied her a minute. She wondered how bad she looked. Her face felt like a mess.

"I have some good news," he announced cheerfully. "The crabs are gone."

Marianne stared at him, wishing him dead. This time he could not hold eye contact. He looked down at the water bottle he held in his hands.

"I…I wanted to apologise for last night. I didn't want to get rough like that. It's just that you forced me to. You and your selfish attitude. I'm not a violent person. I don't hit girls. But you left me with no option. I was only trying to save your life…"

His voice trailed as he turned the bottle over in his hands. Marianne only stared at him, hate and disgust bubbling inside her like a witch's cauldron over a fire. Pain laced her neck and face, and her temple throbbed, but she resisted the urge to lie back down. She drew on her inner reserves. She would not show weakness now or ever again to this fiend.

"You are a lying piece of shit," she hissed between her teeth.

Leigh glanced up, evaluating her. She was too angry to shy away from him now. He had killed her best friend. He had thrown her boyfriend's body to the crabs. And he had beaten her to unconsciousness. What more could he do to her that would be any worse than what he had already done?

"You may think that now, but I saved your life last night. Years from now you will look back on last night and realise that. And then it will be you reaching out to me to apologise."

Marianne scoffed. "You are fucking deluded."

"You can think that all you want. But you owe your life to me. After I fed them, they left us alone. They were too busy taking his body apart to bother us. If you had been awake for it, you would have seen how I saved you."

"Fuck you," Marianne spat. "You only looked after one person. Yourself. Don't try painting it any other way."

He looked at her sadly for a moment. "I'm sorry you see it that way."

He studied her a moment longer before reaching out a hand towards her. She slapped it away weakly.

"Don't touch me," she roared.

"I was only going to help you up."

"I can do it myself."

"Fine. Ungrateful bitch."

Without ceremony, he raised himself up from his haunches and walked out of the tent, taking the water bottle with him. She let her head drop. It had taken all her reserves just to hold herself upright and face him, and the bastard had taken away the water. But she would be damned before letting that beast touch her.

Outside, Leigh resumed his cheerful, tuneless whistling.

After spending a few moments to gather herself, Marianne crawled out of the tent. She knew how pathetic she must have looked, but right now she could not trust herself to stand and walk steadily. Maybe she could achieve it if she rested longer, but the scratching of her throat and dryness of her mouth urged her into action.

She emerged from the tent to the macabre and chaotic scene of the previous night's battle. Broken, dried shells littered the small area they had walled off and defended. The innards of the shells had been picked clean, and only the dull blue-grey shells of those who had been crushed remained.

Leigh had stoked the fire back up and had set up a bubbling pot of water over it. Discarded, empty bottles lay by his feet.

"What are you doing?"

He spoke without looking at her. "Cooking the crab legs and claws of the ones we killed. The other crabs ate all their insides, but I found I could still salvage some meat in the claws and legs."

Marianne's stomach rumbled. She was not sure if she could handle eating crab just now.

"I need water."

"We need to ration it in case Jorge doesn't come."

"I haven't had a drink since last night."

He looked at her, a cynical and condescending look on his face. The reminder that Leigh did not believe Jorge was coming sent shivers through her spine. How did Leigh look upon her right now? Did he really see her as someone he would save from the island, or was she someone he was just saving to be thrown to the crabs the next time they came to keep himself alive a little longer?

"You can have half a cup."

He stood up, and poured her the half cup into a tin coffee mug that had come with the camping gear Jorge had provided. She forced herself into a sitting position and took the cup, draining the liquid slowly and savouring every drop. The cup was empty too quick, and though she yearned for more she kept her wishes to herself.

She looked at the bubbling pot enviously, the precious water within drifting away in clouds of steam.

"Have you checked on Andy this morning?"

He gave her an annoyed and scornful look, as though she had just suggested something despicable.

"No."

Then, as if on cue, they both heard it. The silence of the morning was broken. Andy was screaming.

32

Andy woke with the bright sun already high on the horizon. He blinked slowly, taking time to adjust to the light. He felt weak, despite having had what he thought was a deep and restful sleep. His hair was damp and his back felt wet, and he must have been sweating a lot as he slept.

He rocked his body to the side and raised himself up on his elbow to reach for one of the water bottles. As he did, there was a squelching sound, and his back felt oddly sticky. He was about to reach for the bottle when he saw the crab resting beside it.

The crab noticed him too, instantly rising to its feet and raising its claws aggressively. He waved his hand at it; the little creature responding by snapping its claws and attempting to grab at him.

"Get out of here, you little bugger," he called. The crab stood its ground.

Andy cursed. His t-shirt was wet and clinging to his back uncomfortably in the heat. He reached his arm around to his back to pull the cloth away from his body and allow air in. As he brought his hand back, he noticed his fingers were wet with blood.

"What the f…"

Andy turned and saw what was left of his body for the first time.

The crabs had been busy while Andy had slept. With no feeling below his waist, the sleeping Andy was oblivious to their machinations. The ravenous crabs had fed on him all through the night. At first, they had fed on his feet, chewing the skin away to expose the juicy meat below. There was little to eat on the toes, and soon these were pulled apart and the bones discarded over the edge. The best meat on the feet came when they pulled away the skin of the sole, exposing the meatier flat of the foot and arch.

But not all crabs liked the meat on the feet. Like a family dissecting a roasted chicken, each crab had their own favourite part of the body to devour. More crabs joined the feast, and the sunburnt skin around Andy's calves was quickly stripped away so the crabs could gorge on the soft meat underneath.

Further up Andy's leg, the crabs began scissoring through the muscular flesh of Andy's thighs. Andy and Leigh were both regulars at the gym. Whereas Leigh preferred to lift weights and build muscle (under the belief that girls like muscles and that was how he would win them over), Andy was more of a fitness guy, spending most of his time running or working on the cross-trainer. This gave Andy a very lean body, light on fat but not too tough or overly muscled. The crabs delighted in this, his fitness regime keeping his meat lean and tasty.

The feasting had, of course, caused a lot of bleeding. The natural lay of the ledge pooled the blood under Andy's back, a fact that now drew his attention to their night's gluttony.

For many moments Andy's mind refused to comprehend what he was seeing. Large grey crabs the size of dinner plates hovering all over the lower half of his body, their claws and maws wet with his blood. His skin lay peeled and flayed, lying cruelly discarded around his legs. White bone glistened between the flaps of red flesh that was one of his legs. He watched as one crab flipped his kneecap aside to pull at the delicious tendons underneath. The kneecap skittled along the rock ledge like a thrown pebble. Another crab tore a strip of his hamstring away from the leg, only to scuttle away with his precious meal to eat it alone. A further crab started to pull at the cloth that protected Andy's crotch.

Andy screamed and cursed. Foul language poured from his mouth like a torrent as he shouted every obscenity that came to mind. But if the crabs were offended, they gave no sign of it. Some curious, oval eyes swivelled his way, but mostly the crabs ignored him and continued to gorge on his flesh.

Andy screamed again. Last night he had asked the stars how life could get any worse. The crabs had answered that question in the most brutal way possible.

33

Leigh watched with impassive eyes as Marianne got shakily to her feet. She was a little unsteady, but she was tough. He had to give her that.

"You're not coming to check on your friend?" she asked.

Leigh said nothing. He turned away, stirring the crab claws and legs that bobbed in the pot. Marianne glared at him a few seconds before unleashing a barrage of Dutch at him. Leigh refused to dignify such an outburst, so he ignored her by continuing to stir the brew. She turned and stormed towards the cliff edge.

As Leigh stirred, he started to become aware of a buzzing sound. It struck him immediately as odd. He had not so much as seen a single insect since arriving on the island. He stopped stirring and tilted his head to listen to the sound better.

"Oh god," Marianne cried as she looked over the edge of the cliff.

Leigh turned and scowled in her direction. She had become such an incredible pain in his arse. Dirk must have had the patience of a saint to put up with her all the time.

Marianne then pulled away from the cliff, crawled a few feet and started dry retching on the ground. Leigh rolled his eyes and turned away to focus on the buzzing.

The sound dropped in volume but continued softly humming. Leigh looked in the air about him for the source of the sound, when suddenly it became louder and clearer. It was no insect. It was the sound of an outboard engine.

With rising joy, Leigh turned and rushed to the edge of the cliff to look out over the beach. He spotted the dirty old boat quickly. It was weaving the familiar S shaped curves as it approached the island, dodging the crab's sand bar traps and leaving foamy white water in its wake. The driver was unmistakably aware of the hazards of approaching the island. The driver could only be Jorge.

Elated, Leigh turned to Marianne.

"He's here," he shouted, "Jorge has come to rescue us."

Marianne turned her head to look at him. Rather than bearing the joy at being saved from this island, her face was grim and her eyes were dark.

"Andy needs urgent help," she said, "you will need to get Jorge and bring him up here fast."

Leigh blinked slowly and turned away. He could never understand women. She should be elated right now. Salvation was coming. She and Leigh would be off the island and away from this hell and all she had was dark glares and more orders. Perhaps it was his fault. He had let her lead for a while last night, and now it had gotten to her head. He thought it would be good for her to lead. Empowering even. But she had failed as a leader. She was too weak to make the necessary tough call. If he had continued to let her lead, they would never have given Dirk's corpse to the crabs, and they would never have survived the night.

She should be thankful to him. He took back control and his decisions were what got them through the night. It was regrettable he needed to give her a few taps to make it happen, but as a leader sometimes you needed to do the tough things. He never did any more than what was required at the time.

Marianne crawled back to the edge and leaned over to converse with Andy some more. He could not make out what they were saying, but he could guess. Fucking Andy. He should have known that arsehole would not stop. Even with Inge gone to God knew where, Andy still found another girl to conspire with against him. Who knew what plot was brewing now?

Leigh scowled and stamped forward to pick up his backpack. Out of habit, he picked up Andy's as well.

"I'm going to go meet Jorge," he shouted and turned to stomp down the hill. Marianne turned and shouted something back, but he ignored the remark.

Leigh's mind was again roiling as he stamped his way downhill towards the beach. The bags bumped against his body as he walked, and he stopped halfway down to check his load.

"What the fuck am I carrying Andy's shit for?" he mumbled to himself.

He threw Andy's pack on the ground. The zipper was slightly open, and inside he saw Andy's camera. Leigh stared at it a moment before reaching down to pick it up and switch it on. There was still half a battery remaining.

Leigh looked out to sea. There were still a few minutes before Jorge would make landfall. He turned his attention back to the camera and selected the button to review photos.

The first photos were quite dull. Landscape shots of the beach and of the tents being set up. There was a short video too. Leigh skipped past the video. He knew what it was. It would show Leigh doing all the work to set up the tent while Andy fucked around and filmed them. He did not need to revisit that.

The next set of photos showed Andy up in the ruin. They started normal at first, but as he pushed through them the poses got cheesier and cheesier. Then there were photos of Inge. She was doing sexy poses. Sticking out her chest to accentuate her breasts. Showing her arse to him. Running her tongue across her lips seductively.

He stopped on one photo and ran his fingers over the line of her curves. God how he longed to have touched her. But the photos made him angry. Andy had clearly forced her into these poses, like some sleazy Hollywood casting director. Leigh could picture it all in his head. Andy telling her to pose certain ways, promising her exposure through his huge social following. He probably told her she could be a model. All she needed was the exposure, and he could give that through his social media channels, but only if she returned the favour. Wink, wink. Fucking Andy.

He clicked past the poses, coming to a series of photos of Andy lying on the ledge. Leigh flicked through them quickly. Andy was smiling in some. So much for his broken back.

At last, he came to the final file on the camera. It was a five-minute video. He almost switched the camera off, but a glance seaward showed Jorge would be a little while yet.

He hit play on the video.

Marianne's voice came loudly from the speaker. He turned to look back up the hill, but from this angle he could not see her. He turned back to the vision.

Marianne was retelling the story of the fight in the ruin, but she was not telling it correctly. She was distorting facts. Changing the truth. She was blaming Leigh, saying he had deliberately positioned Andy against the cliff and intended to push Andy over the edge to kill him.

Leigh stopped the video and turned to look back up the hill. His face was screwed up in anger. There was no one there to glare at, so he turned back to the camera.

This was it. This was Andy's final play. A hail Mary pass if ever there was one. He had conspired with Marianne and they had made this video. That was why Marianne had told him this morning to get Jorge and rescue Andy now. They did not want to wait. They were going to accuse Leigh of deliberately pushing Andy over the edge and have him arrested the moment they landed in Bocas Town.

Leigh could not believe it. Fucking Andy and his treacherous bitch Marianne. Andy falling was an accident. He never intended it to happen.

He could not let this video be seen. He clicked delete and wiped it from the camera.

Hearing the engine sputtering, Leigh turned to see Jorge pulling up to the beach.

"Hey," he shouted and waved, "I'm coming."

He left Andy's bag on the ground and broke into a run towards the beach. He slowed as he hit the sand, and as he approached the boat, he eyed the water warily. There were no crabs to be seen.

Jorge greeted him with a curious look and Leigh passed his bag up to be loaded aboard.

"*Donde estan los otros?*" Jorge asked.

Leigh frowned. He had not bothered to learn any Spanish before coming. Jorge seemed to understand and tried again in his limited English.

"Where are others?" he repeated.

Leigh stared at Jorge a moment then turned to look up towards the ruins. He could not see them from this angle, not Marianne at the top nor Andy on his ledge. He turned back to Jorge. Jorge had followed his gaze, but his eyes returned now to meet Leigh's. Jorge gave Leigh a questioning look.

The others. Dirk, dead. Inge, missing and, he presumed, also dead. Andy, paralysed and in need of rescue. Marianne, alive but with her face swollen and bruised.

It was not a good story. Their stay on the island was nothing short of a nightmare. Only Leigh was leaving the island in a relatively good shape. Marianne would recover. Andy possibly could as well.

But the video weighed on Leigh's mind. If there was any indication of what Marianne and Andy intended once they got back to civilisation, it was that video. They would accuse him of pushing Andy deliberately over that cliff. And then there was the mysterious disappearance of Inge. Marianne had already made accusations that he was somehow involved in that. And then there was Dirk. In truth, he had not even checked Dirk's pulse last night. It did not matter, even if Dirk was not already dead, there was no way he was surviving the journey back to Bocas Town. But what if he was still alive the last time Marianne had checked? She could accuse him of throwing a live body to the crabs.

Where did all that leave Leigh? He would be arriving in Bocas Town only to be arrested on charges for two murders, one attempted murder and one assault. They might not find all the evidence directly linking him, but it would come down to Marianne and Andy's word against his. Two against one. Them against him.

But he was not that guy. Leigh was no killer. Andy was an accident, and everything else he had done on the island he had done to survive. Yet it was conceivable, as an act of pure revenge, that Andy and Marianne could conspire it to happen, and Leigh would be forced to spend the rest of his life in some dirty, dangerous Panamanian prison. Or worse, what if Panama still had the death penalty?

No, Leigh thought, I'm not that guy. I did not commit those crimes. I do not deserve to be jailed for them.

Leigh pursed his lips and looked at Jorge once more.

"The others..." he began, before breaking off. He took a deep breath and cleared his throat. "The others are all dead."

34

Marianne pulled away from the ledge to dry retch some more.

The grisly sight of Andy's splayed and ruined body was too much to bear. Those horrible, grey crabs crawling slowly across Andy, their claws and legs dripping with bright crimson blood. Skin, muscle, tissue and tendons were all torn away by the ravenous crabs. Blood pooled around Andy's broken body as the crabs had eaten away his very being all the way through to the bone. Even now the crabs still fed, coldly aware that Andy watched on as they consumed him alive.

When Marianne finally stopped retching, she glanced across the ruin. Leigh had gone, and hopefully he would be back soon with Jorge. They would need to get rope, or make something like one, and haul Andy out of there quickly. Andy was dying, and it was a small window they had to save him.

Catching her breath, Marianne noticed two water bottles lying in the dirt near the fire. She clambered to her feet and staggered towards them. Jorge was here now to take them away, so Leigh can get stuffed if he thinks they still need to ration. Screw him and his 'half a cup only' madness.

She reached the bottles, quickly unscrewing the cap and drinking it down. The water did not sit well in her unsettled stomach, but she had needed the drink badly.

Marianne paused, letting the water sink in as she watched the crab claws and legs bobbing in the boiling water. Yuck. Hopefully Jorge brought some food with him. Otherwise, she would have to wait. She was starving, but she would rather wait until Bocas Town than eat those disgusting crabs.

Marianne took another swig of water and then looked down the hill. What was taking them so long? She had been pretty damn clear in her last instruction to Leigh that he needed to hurry up or Andy would die down there.

Marianne squeezed the bottle, crinkling the plastic in her hand. She began to grow restless. Andy needed help now. She ran to the edge of the cliff that stood over the beach and looked down. She spotted the boat quickly. Leigh sat in the back, beside the smoking and sputtering engine as Jorge pushed it back from the beach.

As Jorge's feet splashed into the shallows, he leapt up onto the boat and crossed it to get behind the wheel to turn the boat around.

"Hey!" Marianne yelled out. "HEY!"

But her yells must have been drowned out by the sound of the motor as neither Jorge nor Leigh looked up. The boat continued to turn, and as it turned away from the island, it accelerated loudly.

"No!" Marianne cried out. She pulled away from the cliff and started running down the hill. Her legs were weak, but driven by desperation she ran and stumbled down the hill towards the beach. She passed Andy's discarded backpack and descended to the flatter part of the island before turning to run onto the beach.

Marianne ran across the sand to the shoreline and shouted to the boat. She started doing star jumps to make herself as big and as visible as she could. The boat turned, and for a second her heart leapt, but as she watched, she realised it was just Jorge turning the boat in one of the S manoeuvres he did about this island. She ran along the beach as fast as she could parallel to the bouncing boat, shouting to draw their attention. The boat turned again, moving farther away from her.

She switched directions, chasing the boat and shouting. But it was no use. The boat was moving farther away with each turn. At last exhaustion overcame her and she stumbled and fell into the sand. She pushed herself up to watch the boat make one last turn away from the island and speed straight out into the open waters of the sea.

For a long time she sat there, watching the boat slowly recede into the distance until it became so small she lost it altogether. She looked back up at the cliffs. Andy would die soon, bleeding out as the crabs continued to feast, and she would be alone. Leigh had saved his most vile and despicable act for last. He had abandoned them, leaving them to die on the island.

Marianne gathered sand into clenched fists and threw the sand into the water. She screamed to the sky. She cursed Leigh and his treacherous, murderous ways. But no tears came. She was well beyond tears now.

The crabs who had gathered along the shoreline watched this show of rage and despair with mirth. They were well satisfied. Most had eaten their fill and sat content in the knowledge they would have food for days to come. There was still meat on the body in the cave and more on the body on the cliff. They could leave this wild, shrieking one for now. Let her live a little longer. Keep her meat fresh. Her turn would come soon enough.

35

Leigh smiled as the wind whipped his face as the boat bounced across the waves. Free at last!

It had been a hellish couple of days on Crab Island, or Blue Island, or whatever the fuck it was called, but he had made it. Andy had been right all along. Crab Island was the most extreme adventure around. It was dangerous, it was creepy, and it was quite unlike anything else in the world. He was right to seek it out. It would have made one hell of a story on social media. It was the ultimate experience. And Leigh had survived.

Leigh leaned back and relaxed. He should feel proud at what he had achieved. Crab Island was secret for a reason. It was frightening and deadly, and he was now part of an elite group of survivors. He doubted there would be many other people who had camped there and lived to tell the tale.

Leigh shifted position on the seat. Something in his pocket was digging uncomfortably into his thigh. He pushed his hand into his pocket to retrieve the annoyance. It was the keyring Inge had given him three days earlier.

Leigh held it out in front of him and studied it. Inge had loved him. He knew it was true, and this gift proved it. He should be with Inge now. She should be sitting here beside him. Leigh would have his arm resting across her shoulder and she would be looking up at him and smiling.

Andy had ruined all that. He had stuck his fat nose in and ruined it for Leigh as he always did.

Leigh cast the keyring over the side of the boat. It was over now, and he was over Inge. They would never come to be, and he accepted that now.

Leigh turned and looked back at the island one last time. They were quite distant, but he was sure he could see movement on the beach. He turned away. He could not feel guilt over the decision he had made. Leigh did not deserve a life in prison, and neither Andy nor Marianne had the right to do that to him. They forced his hand on the issue. His decision to leave them behind was on them.

As he turned away, the engine started to sputter and died. Leigh rolled his eyes. Not this again. Jorge needed to do himself a favour and spend all the money he earned off this trip on a new engine or a good mechanic. Any more of this and Jorge would end up stranded adrift in the middle of the Caribbean Sea.

Leigh reached down to pick up Andy's camera once more. He would delete all the photos. Clear any and all evidence of him ever being on Crab Island. If people asked, he could tell them Andy found the island and went there alone. Or better yet, met some Dutch travellers and went there with them. Andy's family would ask. There might be an investigation. He could free himself from all of that, he just needed to destroy the evidence.

Leigh was so deeply caught up in his final trickery that he failed to notice Jorge's movements.

"Hey, gringo," Jorge called.

Leigh looked up from the camera. He barely had time to process what he saw: Jorge pointing a gun in his direction. Then the world went black.

36

The bullet that hit Leigh shattered through his eye socket and exploded out of the other side of his head, killing him instantly. Blood and skull fragments splashed into the water behind where he sat and floated away in a red cloud. Jorge stared at the body a moment before he stowed the gun and turned to deal with the body.

The sea around him was empty for miles. He doubted the shot would be heard, and even if it was, he would be long gone before anyone arrived.

He lifted and pushed Leigh's dead body over the side of the boat. The camera clattered to the floor. Jorge picked it up and examined it, before stowing it away as well. He could clean it and sell it later. It would make up for the money he lost on the camping equipment.

Jorge quickly cleaned the boat of blood. He sorted through Leigh's possessions for anything he could use or sell, before turfing this over the side as well.

Finally, Jorge slumped into the seat and looked back in the direction of *Isla Azul*. He shook his head sadly. More deaths. How many had died there now? Too many. It was a sad business, but the more people disappeared due to the island, the more its legend grew. He had to stop taking curious travellers there. It never ended well, and soon authorities would tire of the countless missing person cases and finally get off their lazy arses and investigate. An investigation that, if they did their jobs right, would lead straight to him.

Which was why Jorge could not leave any loose ends. No lone survivors to tell the story and point their finger at him. Too many had died and they would scapegoat him into responsibility. He had taken them all out there, after all.

But Jorge never saw himself at fault. If people wanted to kill themselves, then let them. He had warned that man, what was his name… Andy? He had warned him of the danger, but Andy only upped his offer. How could Jorge refuse after being offered one thousand US dollars? Jorge had six children and two ex-wives to support. One thousand dollars was a good haul for a boat ride and camping rental. And besides, that gringo was so desperate to go to the island, if Jorge had not taken him, someone else would have anyway.

But one thousand dollars was nothing compared to the loss of four young lives. Well, five now. He regretted having to kill that last boy, but the risk of what he might say to the police was too high. If that gringo Andy had survived, he would have let them go happily. He had told Andy all the risks and they even had a signed contract, there was no way Andy could make him culpable. But the contract only existed for Andy. He had forgotten to get it from the others. He had no idea what this boy might say, and he could blame Jorge for everything. He could say Jorge had taken them there and never explained the danger, and they could lock Jorge away for it.

Jorge cursed himself for the error. He sat a while as the boat rocked gently on the waves and prayed for the lives that were lost.

Eventually Jorge stood and went to restart the engine. He had to stop bringing people to the island. The risk was too great. Too many died on that hellish island.

Jorge resumed his seat at the wheel and pushed the throttle forward, vowing never again to return to the island of the crabs.

The End

@severedpress
/severedpress

Check out other great

Sea Monster Novels!

Robert J. Stava

NEPTUNES RECKONING

At the easternmost end of Long Island lies a seaside town known as Montauk. Ground Zero on the Eastern seaboard for all manner of conspiracy theories involving it's hidden Cold War military base, rumors of time-travel experiments and alien visitors... For renowned Naval historian William Vanek it's the where his grandfather's ship went down on a Top Secret mission during WWII code-named "Neptune's Reckoning". Together with Marine Biologist Daniel Cheung and disgraced French underwater explorer Arnaud Navarre, he's about to discover the truth behind the urban legends: a nightmare from beyond space and time that has been reawakened by global warming and toxic dumping, a nightmare the government tried to keep submerged. Neptune's Reckoning. Terror knows no depth

Bestselling collection

DEAD BAIT

A husband hell-bent on revenge hunts a Wereshark... A Russian mail order bride with a fishy secret... Crabs with a collective consciousness... A vampire who transforms into a Candiru... Zombie piranha...Bait that will have you crawling out of your skin and more. Drawing on horror, humor with a helping of dark fantasy and a touch of deviance, these 19 contemporary stories pay homage to the monsters that lurk in the murky waters of our imaginations. If you thought it was safe to go back in the water... Think Again!

www.ingramcontent.com/pod-product-compliance
Lightning Source LLC
LaVergne TN
LVHW091146080826
845145LV00008B/2273